The Spoken Word of Jesus Christ

Published by New Generation Publishing in 2012

www.newgeneration-publishing.com

 New Generation Publishing

Matthew

Matthew 3

The Baptism of Jesus

15 And Jesus answering said unto him, Suffer *it to be so* now: for thus it becometh us to fulfil all righteousness.

Matthew 4

The Temptation of Jesus

3 And when the tempter came to him, he said, If thou be the Son of God, command that these stones be made bread. 4 But he answered and said, It is written, **Man shall not live by bread alone, but by every word that proceedeth out of the mouth of God.** 5 Then the devil taketh him up into the holy city, and setteth him on a pinnacle of the temple, 6 And saith unto him, If thou be the Son of God, cast thyself down: for it is written, **He shall give his angels charge concerning thee: and in** *their* **hands they shall bear thee up, lest at any time thou dash thy foot against a stone.** 7 Jesus said unto him, It is written again, **Thou shalt not tempt the Lord thy God.** 8 Again, the devil taketh him up into an exceeding high mountain, and sheweth him all the kingdoms of the world, and the glory of them; 9 And saith unto him, All these things will I give thee, if thou wilt fall down and worship me. 10 Then saith Jesus unto him, Get thee hence, Satan: for it is written, **Thou shalt worship the Lord thy God, and him only shalt thou serve.**

The Preaching Ministry of Jesus

17 From that time Jesus began to preach, and to say, Repent: for the kingdom of heaven is at hand.

The Call of the Disciples
19 And he saith unto them, Follow me, and I will make you fishers of men.

Matthew 5

The Beatitudes
3 Blessed *are* the poor in spirit: for theirs is the kingdom of heaven. **4** Blessed *are* they that mourn: for they shall be comforted. **5** Blessed *are* the meek: for they shall inherit the earth. **6** Blessed *are* they which do hunger and thirst after righteousness: for they shall be filled. **7** Blessed *are* the merciful: for they shall obtain mercy. **8** Blessed *are* the pure in heart: for they shall see God. **9** Blessed *are* the peacemakers: for they shall be called the children of God. **10** Blessed *are* they which are persecuted for righteousness' sake: for theirs is the kingdom of heaven. **11** Blessed are ye, when *men* shall revile you, and persecute *you*, and shall say all manner of evil against you falsely, for my sake. **12** Rejoice, and be exceeding glad: for great *is* your reward in heaven: for so persecuted they the prophets which were before you.

Salt and Light
13 Ye are the salt of the earth: but if the salt have lost his savour, wherewith shall it be salted? it is thenceforth good for nothing, but to be cast out, and to be trodden under foot of men. **14** Ye are the light of the world. A city that is set on an hill cannot be hid. **15** Neither do men light a candle, and put it under a bushel, but on a candlestick; and it giveth light unto all that are in the house. **16** Let your light so shine before men, that they may see your good works, and glorify your Father which is in heaven.

Fulfilment of the Law and Prophets

17 Think not that I am come to destroy the law, or the prophets: I am not come to destroy, but to fulfil. **18** For verily I say unto you, Till heaven and earth pass, one jot or one tittle shall in no wise pass from the law, till all be fulfilled. **19** Whosoever therefore shall break one of these least commandments, and shall teach men so, he shall be called the least in the kingdom of heaven: but whosoever shall do and teach *them*, the same shall be called great in the kingdom of heaven. **20** For I say unto you, That except your righteousness shall exceed *the righteousness* of the scribes and Pharisees, ye shall in no case enter into the kingdom of heaven.

Teachings on Murder and Anger

21 Ye have heard that it was said by them of old time, Thou shalt not kill; and whosoever shall kill shall be in danger of the judgment: **22** But I say unto you, That whosoever is angry with his brother without a cause shall be in danger of the judgment: and whosoever shall say to his brother, Raca, shall be in danger of the council: but whosoever shall say, Thou fool, shall be in danger of hell fire. **23** Therefore if thou bring thy gift to the altar, and there rememberest that thy brother hath ought against thee; **24** Leave there thy gift before the altar, and go thy way; first be reconciled to thy brother, and then come and offer thy gift. **25** Agree with thine adversary quickly, whiles thou art in the way with him; lest at any time the adversary deliver thee to the judge, and the judge deliver thee to the officer, and thou be cast into prison. **26** Verily I say unto thee, Thou shalt by no means come out thence, till thou hast paid the uttermost farthing.

Teachings on Temptation

27 Ye have heard that it was said by them of old time, Thou shalt not commit adultery: **28** But I say unto you, That whosoever looketh on a woman to lust after her hath committed adultery with her already in his heart. **29** And if thy right eye offend thee, pluck it out, and cast *it* from thee: for it is profitable for thee that one of thy members should perish, and not *that* thy whole body should be cast into hell. **30** And if thy right hand offend thee, cut it off, and cast *it* from thee: for it is profitable for thee that one of thy members should perish, and not *that* thy whole body should be cast into hell.

Teachings on Divorce
31 It hath been said, Whosoever shall put away his wife, let him give her a writing of divorcement: **32** But I say unto you, That whosoever shall put away his wife, saving for the cause of fornication, causeth her to commit adultery: and whosoever shall marry her that is divorced committeth adultery.

Teachings on Oaths
33 Again, ye have heard that it hath been said by them of old time, Thou shalt not forswear thyself, but shalt perform unto the Lord thine oaths: **34** But I say unto you, Swear not at all; neither by heaven; for it is God's throne: **35** Nor by the earth; for it is his footstool: neither by Jerusalem; for it is the city of the great King. **36** Neither shalt thou swear by thy head, because thou canst not make one hair white or black. **37** But let your communication be, Yea, yea; Nay, nay: for whatsoever is more than these cometh of evil.

Teachings on Forgiveness
38 Ye have heard that it hath been said, An eye for an eye, and a tooth for a tooth: **39** But I say unto you, That ye resist not evil: but whosoever shall smite thee on thy right cheek, turn to him the other also. **40** And if any man will sue thee at the law, and take away thy coat, let him have *thy* cloke also. **41** And whosoever shall compel thee to go a mile, go with him twain. **42** Give to him that asketh thee, and from him that would borrow of thee turn not thou away.

Teachings on Loving One's Enemies

43 Ye have heard that it hath been said, Thou shalt love thy neighbour, and hate thine enemy. **44** But I say unto you, Love your enemies, bless them that curse you, do good to them that hate you, and pray for them which despitefully use you, and persecute you; **45** That ye may be the children of your Father which is in heaven: for he maketh his sun to rise on the evil and on the good, and sendeth rain on the just and on the unjust. **46** For if ye love them which love you, what reward have ye? do not even the publicans the same? **47** And if ye salute your brethren only, what do ye more *than others*? do not even the publicans so? **48** Be ye therefore perfect, even as your Father which is in heaven is perfect.

Matthew 6

Teachings on Giving

1 Take heed that ye do not your alms before men, to be seen of them: otherwise ye have no reward of your Father which is in heaven. **2** Therefore when thou doest *thine* alms, do not sound a trumpet before thee, as the hypocrites do in the synagogues and in the streets, that they may have glory of men. Verily I say unto you, They have their reward. **3** But when thou doest alms, let not thy left hand know what thy right hand doeth: **4** That thine alms may be in secret: and thy Father which seeth in secret himself shall reward thee openly.

Teachings on Prayer

5 And when thou prayest, thou shalt not be as the hypocrites *are*: for they love to pray standing in the synagogues and in the corners of the streets, that they may be seen of men. Verily I say unto you, They have their reward. **6** But thou, when thou prayest, enter into thy closet, and when thou hast shut thy door, pray to thy Father which is in secret; and thy Father which seeth in secret shall reward thee openly. **7** But when ye pray, use not vain repetitions, as the heathen *do*: for they think that they shall be heard for their much speaking. **8** Be not ye therefore like unto them: for your Father knoweth what things ye have need of, before ye ask him.

9 After this manner therefore pray ye: Our Father which art in heaven, Hallowed be thy name. **10** Thy kingdom come. Thy will be done in earth, as *it is* in heaven. **11** Give us this day our daily bread. **12** And forgive us our debts, as we forgive our debtors. **13** And lead us not into temptation, but deliver us from evil: For thine is the kingdom, and the power, and the glory, forever. Amen. **14** For if ye forgive men their trespasses, your heavenly Father will also forgive you: **15** But if ye forgive not men their trespasses, neither will your Father forgive your trespasses.

Teachings on Fasting

16 Moreover when ye fast, be not, as the hypocrites, of a sad countenance: for they disfigure their faces, that they may appear unto men to fast. Verily I say unto you, They have their reward. **17** But thou, when thou fastest, anoint thine head, and wash thy face; **18** That thou appear not unto men to fast, but unto thy Father which is in secret: and thy Father, which seeth in secret, shall reward thee openly.

Teachings on Treasures in Heaven

19 Lay not up for yourselves treasures upon earth, where moth and rust doth corrupt, and where thieves break through and steal: **20** But lay up for yourselves treasures in heaven, where neither moth nor rust doth corrupt, and where thieves do not break through nor steal: **21** For where your treasure is, there will your heart be also. **22** The light of the body is the eye: if therefore thine eye be single, thy whole body shall be full of light. **23** But if thine eye be evil, thy whole body shall be full of darkness. If therefore the light that is in thee be darkness, how great *is* that darkness! **24** No man can serve two masters: for either he will hate the one, and love the other; or else he will hold to the one, and despise the other. Ye cannot serve God and mammon.

Teachings on Worry

25 Therefore I say unto you, Take no thought for your life, what ye shall eat, or what ye shall drink; nor yet for your body, what ye shall put on. Is not the life more than meat, and the body than raiment? **26** Behold the fowls of the air: for they sow not, neither do they reap, nor gather into barns; yet your heavenly Father feedeth them. Are ye not much better than they? **27** Which of you by taking thought can add one cubit unto his stature? **28** And why take ye thought for raiment? Consider the lilies of the field, how they grow; they toil not, neither do they spin: **29** And yet I say unto you, That even Solomon in all his glory was not arrayed like one of these. **30** Wherefore, if God so clothe the grass of the field, which today is, and tomorrow is cast into the oven, *shall he* not much more *clothe* you, O ye of little faith? **31** Therefore take no thought, saying, What shall we eat? or, What shall we drink? or, Wherewithal shall we be clothed? **32** (For after all these things do the Gentiles seek:) for your heavenly Father knoweth that ye have need of all these things. **33** But seek ye first the kingdom of God, and his righteousness; and all these things shall be added unto you. **34** Take therefore no thought for the morrow: for the morrow shall take thought for the things of itself. Sufficient unto the day *is* the evil thereof.

Matthew 7

Judging and Being Judged

1 Judge not, that ye be not judged. **2** For with what judgment ye judge, ye shall be judged: and with what measure ye mete, it shall be measured to you again. **3** And why beholdest thou the mote that is in thy brother's eye, but considerest not the beam that is in thine own eye? **4** Or how wilt thou say to thy brother, Let me pull out the mote out of thine eye; and, behold, a beam *is* in thine own eye? **5** Thou hypocrite, first cast out the beam out of thine own eye; and then shalt thou see clearly to cast out the mote out of thy brother's eye. **6** Give not that which is holy unto the dogs, neither cast ye your pearls before swine, lest they trample them under their feet, and turn again and rend you.

Ask, Seek, Knock
7 Ask, and it shall be given you; seek, and ye shall find; knock, and it shall be opened unto you: **8** For every one that asketh receiveth; and he that seeketh findeth; and to him that knocketh it shall be opened. **9** Or what man is there of you, whom if his son ask bread, will he give him a stone? **10** Or if he ask a fish, will he give him a serpent? **11** If ye then, being evil, know how to give good gifts unto your children, how much more shall your Father which is in heaven give good things to them that ask him?
12 Therefore all things whatsoever ye would that men should do to you, do ye even so to them: for this is the law and the prophets.

The Strait and Wide Gates
13 Enter ye in at the strait gate: for wide *is* the gate, and broad *is* the way, that leadeth to destruction, and many there be which go in thereat: **14** Because strait *is* the gate, and narrow *is* the way, which leadeth unto life, and few there be that find it.

False Prophets
15 Beware of false prophets, which come to you in sheep's clothing, but inwardly they are ravening wolves. **16** Ye shall know them by their fruits. Do men gather grapes of thorns, or figs of thistles? **17** Even so every good tree bringeth forth good fruit; but a corrupt tree bringeth forth evil fruit. **18** A good tree cannot bring forth evil fruit, neither *can* a corrupt tree bring forth good fruit. **19** Every tree that bringeth not forth good fruit is hewn down, and cast into the fire. **20** Wherefore by their fruits ye shall know them.

21 Not everyone that saith unto me, Lord, Lord, shall enter into the kingdom of heaven; but he that doeth the will of my Father which is in heaven. **22** Many will say to me in that day, Lord, Lord, have we not prophesied in thy name? and in thy name have cast out devils? and in thy name done many wonderful works? **23** And then will I profess unto them, I never knew you: depart from me, ye that work iniquity.

Rock or Sand Foundations

24 Therefore whosoever heareth these sayings of mine, and doeth them, I will liken him unto a wise man, which built his house upon a rock: **25** And the rain descended, and the floods came, and the winds blew, and beat upon that house; and it fell not: for it was founded upon a rock. **26** And every one that heareth these sayings of mine, and doeth them not, shall be likened unto a foolish man, which built his house upon the sand: **27** And the rain descended, and the floods came, and the winds blew, and beat upon that house; and it fell: and great was the fall of it.

Matthew 8

Jesus Heals a Leper

3 And Jesus put forth *his* hand, and touched him, saying, I will; be thou clean. And immediately his leprosy was cleansed. **4** And Jesus saith unto him, See thou tell no man; but go thy way, shew thyself to the priest, and offer the gift that Moses commanded, for a testimony unto them.

A Centurion's Faith

5 And when Jesus was entered into Capernaum, there came unto him a centurion, beseeching him, **6** And saying, Lord, my servant lieth at home sick of the palsy, grievously tormented. **7** And Jesus saith unto him, I will come and heal him. **8** The centurion answered and said, Lord, I am not worthy that thou shouldest come under my roof: but speak the word only, and my servant shall be healed. **9** For I am a man under authority, having soldiers under me: and I say to this man, Go, and he goeth; and to another, Come, and he cometh; and to my servant, Do this, and he doeth it. **10** When Jesus heard it, he marvelled, and said to them that followed, Verily I say unto you, I have not found so great faith, no, not in Israel. **11** And I say unto you, That many shall come from the east and west, and shall sit down with Abraham, and Isaac, and Jacob, in the kingdom of heaven. **12** But the children of the kingdom shall be cast out into outer darkness: there shall be weeping and gnashing of teeth. **13** And Jesus said unto the centurion, Go thy way; and as thou hast believed, so be it done unto thee.

The Cost of Discipleship

19 And a certain scribe came, and said unto him, Master, I will follow thee whithersoever thou goest. **20** And Jesus saith unto him, The foxes have holes, and the birds of the air have nests; but the Son of man hath not where to lay his head. **21** And another of his disciples said unto him, Lord, suffer me first to go and bury my father. **22** But Jesus said unto him, Follow me; and let the dead bury their dead. **26** And he saith unto them, Why are ye fearful, O ye of little faith?

Matthew 9

Healing a Man with Palsy

2 And, behold, they brought to him a man sick of the palsy, lying on a bed: and Jesus seeing their faith said unto the sick of the palsy; Son, be of good cheer; thy sins be forgiven thee. **4** And Jesus knowing their thoughts said, Wherefore think ye evil in your hearts? **5** For whether is easier, to say, Thy sins be forgiven thee; or to say, Arise, and walk? **6** But that ye may know that the Son of man hath power on earth to forgive sins, (then saith he to the sick of the palsy,) Arise, take up thy bed, and go unto thine house.

The Call of Matthew; Eating with Sinners

9 And as Jesus passed forth from thence, he saw a man, named Matthew, sitting at the receipt of custom: and he saith unto him, Follow me. And he arose, and followed him. **12** But when Jesus heard that, he said unto them, They that be whole need not a physician, but they that are sick. **13** But go ye and learn what that meaneth, **I will have mercy, and not sacrifice:** for I am not come to call the righteous, but sinners to repentance.

Questions about Fasting

14 Then came to him the disciples of John, saying, Why do we and the Pharisees fast oft, but thy disciples fast not? **15** And Jesus said unto them, Can the children of the bridechamber mourn, as long as the bridegroom is with them? but the days will come, when the bridegroom shall be taken from them, and then shall they fast. **16** No man putteth a piece of new cloth unto an old garment, for that which is put in to fill it up taketh from the garment, and the rent is made worse. **17** Neither do men put new wine into old bottles: else the bottles break, and the wine runneth out, and the bottles perish: but they put new wine into new bottles, and both are preserved.*²*

Restoration and Healing

22 But Jesus turned him about, and when he saw her, he said, Daughter, be of good comfort; thy faith hath made thee whole. And the woman was made whole from that hour. **23** And when Jesus came into the ruler's house, and saw the minstrels and the people making a noise, **24** He said unto them, Give place: for the maid is not dead, but sleepeth. And they laughed him to scorn. **25** But when the people were put forth, he went in, and took her by the hand, and the maid arose.

Healing the Blind and Mute

28 And when he was come into the house, the blind men came to him: and Jesus saith unto them, Believe ye that I am able to do this? They said unto him, Yea, Lord. **29** Then touched he their eyes, saying, According to your faith be it unto you. **30** And their eyes were opened; and Jesus straitly charged them, saying, See *that* no man know *it.*

Labourers for the Harvest

37 Then saith he unto his disciples, The harvest truly is plenteous, but the labourers are few; **38** Pray ye therefore the Lord of the harvest, that he will send forth labourers into his harvest.

Matthew 10

Sending Out the Twelve Apostles

5 These twelve Jesus sent forth, and commanded them, saying, Go not into the way of the Gentiles, and into *any* city of the Samaritans enter ye not: **6** But go rather to the lost sheep of the house of Israel. **7** And as ye go, preach, saying, The kingdom of heaven is at hand. **8** Heal the sick, cleanse the lepers, raise the dead, cast out devils: freely ye have received, freely give. **9** Provide neither gold, nor silver, nor brass in your purses, **10** Nor scrip for *your* journey, neither two coats, neither shoes, nor yet staves: for the workman is worthy of his meat. **11** And into whatsoever city or town ye shall enter, enquire who in it is worthy; and there abide till ye go thence. **12** And when ye come into an house, salute it. **13** And if the house be worthy, let your peace come upon it: but if it be not worthy, let your peace return to you. **14** And whosoever shall not receive you, nor hear your words, when ye depart out of that house or city, shake off the dust of your feet. **15** Verily I say unto you, It shall be more tolerable for the land of Sodom and Gomorrha in the day of judgment, than for that city.

Sheep among Wolves

16 Behold, I send you forth as sheep in the midst of wolves: be ye therefore wise as serpents, and harmless as doves. **17** But beware of men: for they will deliver you up to the councils, and they will scourge you in their synagogues; **18** And ye shall be brought before governors and kings for my sake, for a testimony against them and the Gentiles. **19** But when they deliver you up, take no thought how or what ye shall speak: for it shall be given you in that same hour what ye shall speak. **20** For it is not ye that speak, but the Spirit of your Father which speaketh in you. **21** And the brother shall deliver up the brother to death, and the father the child: and the children shall rise up against *their* parents, and cause them to be put to death. **22** And ye shall be hated of all *men* for my name's sake: but he that endureth to the end shall be saved. **23** But when they persecute you in this city, flee ye into another: for verily I say unto you, Ye shall not have gone over the cities of Israel, till the Son of man be come. **24** The disciple is not above *his* master, nor the servant above his lord. **25** It is enough for the disciple that he be as his master, and the servant as his lord. If they have called the master of the house Beelzebub, how much more *shall they call* them of his household? **26** Fear them not therefore: for there is nothing covered, that shall not be revealed; and hid, that shall not be known. **27** What I tell you in darkness, *that* speak ye in light: and what ye hear in the ear, *that* preach ye upon the housetops. **28** And fear not them which kill the body, but are not able to kill the soul: but rather fear him which is able to destroy both soul and body in hell. **29** Are not two sparrows sold for a farthing? and one of them shall not fall on the ground without your Father.⁷ **30** But the very hairs of your head are all numbered. **31** Fear ye not therefore, ye are of more value than many sparrows. **32** Whosoever therefore shall confess me before men, him will I confess also before my Father which is in heaven. **33** But whosoever shall deny me before men, him will I also deny before my Father which is in heaven. **34** Think not that I am come to send peace on earth: I came not to send peace, but a sword. **35** **For I am come to set a man at variance against his father, and the daughter against her mother, and the daughter in law against her mother in law. 36 And a** man's foes *shall be* **they of his own household.** **37** He that loveth father or mother more than me is not worthy of me: and he that loveth son or daughter more than me is not worthy of me. **38** And he that taketh not his cross, and followeth after me, is not worthy of me. **39** He that findeth his life shall lose it: and he that loseth his life for my sake shall find it. **40** He that receiveth you receiveth me, and he that receiveth me receiveth him that sent me. **41** He that receiveth a prophet in the name of a prophet shall receive a prophet's reward; and he that receiveth a righteous man in the name of a righteous man shall receive a righteous man's reward. **42** And whosoever shall give to drink unto one of these little ones a cup of cold *water* only in the name of a disciple, verily I say unto you, he shall in no wise lose his reward.

Matthew 11

John's Questions for Jesus

4 Jesus answered and said unto them, Go and shew John again those things which ye do hear and see: **5** The blind receive their sight, and the lame walk, the lepers are cleansed, and the deaf hear, the dead are raised up, and the poor have the gospel preached to them. **6** And blessed is *he*, whosoever shall not be offended in me.

7 And as they departed, Jesus began to say unto the multitudes concerning John, What went ye out into the wilderness to see? A reed shaken with the wind? **8** But what went ye out for to see? A man clothed in soft raiment? behold, they that wear soft *clothing* are in kings' houses. **9** But what went ye out for to see? A prophet? yea, I say unto you, and more than a prophet. **10** For this is *he*, of whom it is written, **Behold, I send my messenger before thy face, which shall prepare thy way before thee.** **11** Verily I say unto you, Among them that are born of women there hath not risen a greater than John the Baptist: notwithstanding he that is least in the kingdom of heaven is greater than he. **12** And from the days of John the Baptist until now the kingdom of heaven suffereth violence, and the violent take it by force. **13** For all the prophets and the law prophesied until John. **14** And if ye will receive *it*, this is Elias, which was for to come. **15** He that hath ears to hear, let him hear.

16 But whereunto shall I liken this generation? It is like unto children sitting in the markets, and calling unto their fellows, **17** And saying, We have piped unto you, and ye have not danced; we have mourned unto you, and ye have not lamented. **18** For John came neither eating nor drinking, and they say, He hath a devil. **19** The Son of man came eating and drinking, and they say, Behold a man gluttonous, and a winebibber, a friend of publicans and sinners. But wisdom is justified of her children.

Unrepentant Cities

20 Then began he to upbraid the cities wherein most of his mighty works were done, because they repented not: **21** Woe unto thee, Chorazin! woe unto thee, Bethsaida! for if the mighty works, which were done in you, had been done in Tyre and Sidon, they would have repented long ago in sackcloth and ashes. **22** But I say unto you, It shall be more tolerable for Tyre and Sidon at the day of judgment, than for you. **23** And thou, Capernaum, which art exalted unto heaven, shalt be brought down to hell: for if the mighty works, which have been done in thee, had been done in Sodom, it would have remained until this day. **24** But I say unto you, That it shall be more tolerable for the land of Sodom in the day of judgment, than for thee.

Jesus' Invitation: Rest for the Heavy Laden

25 At that time Jesus answered and said, I thank thee, O Father, Lord of heaven and earth, because thou hast hid these things from the wise and prudent, and hast revealed them unto babes. **26** Even so, Father: for so it seemed good in thy sight. **27** All things are delivered unto me of my Father: and no man knoweth the Son, but the Father; neither knoweth any man the Father, save the Son, and *he* to whomsoever the Son will reveal *him*. **28**

Come unto me, all *ye* that labour and are heavy laden, and I will give you rest. **29** Take my yoke upon you, and learn of me; for I am meek and lowly in heart: and ye shall find rest unto your souls. **30** For my yoke *is* easy, and my burden is light.

Matthew 12

Lord of the Sabbath

3 But he said unto them, Have ye not read what David did, when he was an hungred, and they that were with him; **4** How he entered into the house of God, and did eat the shewbread, which was not lawful for him to eat, neither for them which were with him, but only for the priests? **5** Or have ye not read in the law, how that on the sabbath days the priests in the temple profane the sabbath, and are blameless? **6** But I say unto you, That in this place is *one* greater than the temple. **7** But if ye had known what *this* meaneth, I will have mercy, and not sacrifice, ye would not have condemned the guiltless. **8** For the Son of man is Lord even of the sabbath day.

11 And he said unto them, What man shall there be among you, that shall have one sheep, and if it fall into a pit on the sabbath day, will he not lay hold on it, and lift *it* out? **12** How much then is a man better than a sheep? Wherefore it is lawful to do well on the sabbath days. **13** Then saith he to the man, Stretch forth thine hand. And he stretched *it* forth; and it was restored whole, like as the other.

Jesus: Of Beelzebul or God?

25 And Jesus knew their thoughts, and said unto them, Every kingdom divided against itself is brought to desolation; and every city or house divided against itself shall not stand: **26** And if Satan cast out Satan, he is divided against himself; how shall then his kingdom stand? **27** And if I by Beelzebub cast out devils, by whom do your children cast *them* out? therefore they shall be your judges. **28** But if I cast out devils by the Spirit of God, then the kingdom of God is come unto you. **29** Or else how can one enter into a strong man's house, and spoil his goods, except he first bind the strong man? and then he will spoil his house. **30** He that is not with me is against me; and he that gathereth not with me scattereth abroad. **31** Wherefore I say unto you, All manner of sin and blasphemy shall be forgiven unto men: but the blasphemy *against* the *Holy* Ghost shall not be forgiven unto men. **32** And whosoever speaketh a word against the Son of man, it shall be forgiven him: but whosoever speaketh against the Holy Ghost, it shall not be forgiven him, neither in this world, neither in the *world* to come. **33** Either make the tree good, and his fruit good; or else make the tree corrupt, and his fruit corrupt: for the tree is known by *his* fruit. **34** O generation of vipers, how can ye, being evil, speak good things? for out of the abundance of the heart the mouth speaketh. **35** A good man out of the good treasure of the heart bringeth forth good things: and an evil man out of the evil treasure bringeth forth evil things. **36** But I say unto you, That every idle word that men shall speak, they shall give account thereof in the day of judgment. **37** For by thy words thou shalt be justified, and by thy words thou shalt be condemned.

The Sign of the Prophet

39 But he answered and said unto them, An evil and adulterous generation seeketh after a sign; and there shall no sign be given to it, but the sign of the prophet Jonas: **40** For as Jonas was three days and three nights in the whale's belly; so shall the Son of man be three days and three nights in the heart of the earth. **41** The men of Nineveh shall rise in judgment with this generation, and shall condemn it: because they repented at the preaching of Jonas; and, behold, a greater than Jonas *is* here. **42** The queen of the south shall rise up in the judgment with this generation, and shall condemn it: for she came from the uttermost parts of the earth to hear the wisdom of Solomon; and, behold, a greater than Solomon *is* here. **43** When the unclean spirit is gone out of a man, he walketh through dry places, seeking rest, and findeth none. **44** Then he saith, I will return into my house from whence I came out; and when he is come, he findeth it empty, swept, and garnished. **45** Then goeth he, and taketh with himself seven other spirits more wicked than himself, and they enter in and dwell there: and the last *state* of that man is worse than the first. Even so shall it be also unto this wicked generation.

The Family of Jesus

48 But he answered and said unto him that told him, Who is my mother? and who are my brethren? **49** And he stretched forth his hand toward his disciples, and said, Behold my mother and my brethren! **50** For whosoever shall do the will of my Father which is in heaven, the same is my brother, and sister, and mother.

Matthew 13

The Parable of the Sower

3 And he spake many things unto them in parables, saying, Behold, a sower went forth to sow; **4** And when he sowed, some *seeds* fell by the way side, and the fowls came and devoured them up: **5** Some fell upon stony places, where they had not much earth: and forthwith they sprung up, because they had no deepness of earth: **6** And when the sun was up, they were scorched; and because they had no root, they withered away. **7** And some fell among thorns; and the thorns sprung up, and choked them: **8** But other fell into good ground, and brought forth fruit, some an hundredfold, some sixtyfold, some thirtyfold. **9** Who hath ears to hear, let him hear. **10** And the disciples came, and said unto him, Why speakest thou unto them in parables? **11** He answered and said unto them, Because it is given unto you to know the mysteries of the kingdom of heaven, but to them it is not given. **12** For whosoever hath, to him shall be given, and he shall have more abundance: but whosoever hath not, from him shall be taken away even that he hath. **13**

Therefore speak I to them in parables: because they seeing see not; and hearing they hear not, neither do they understand. **14** And in them is fulfilled the prophecy of Esaias, which saith, **By hearing ye shall hear, and shall not understand; and seeing ye shall see, and shall not perceive: 15 For this people's heart is waxed gross, and** *their* **ears are dull of hearing, and their eyes they have closed; lest at any time they should see with** *their* **eyes, and hear with** *their* **ears, and should understand with** *their* **heart, and should be converted, and I should heal them.** **16** But blessed *are* your eyes, for they see: and your ears, for they hear. **17** For verily I say unto you, That many prophets and righteous *men* have desired to see *those things* which ye see, and have not seen *them*; and to hear *those things* which ye hear, and have not heard *them*. **18** Hear ye therefore the parable of the sower. **19** When any one heareth the word of the kingdom, and understandeth *it* not, then cometh the wicked *one*, and catcheth away that which was sown in his heart. This is he which received seed by the way side. **20** But he that received the seed into stony places, the same is he that heareth the word, and anon with joy receiveth it; **21** Yet hath he not root in himself, but dureth for a while: for when tribulation or persecution ariseth because of the word, by and by he is offended. **22** He also that received seed among the thorns is he that heareth the word; and the care of this world, and the deceitfulness of riches, choke the word, and he becometh unfruitful. **23** But he that received seed into the good ground is he that heareth the word, and understandeth *it*; which also beareth fruit, and bringeth forth, some an hundredfold, some sixty, some thirty.

The Parable of the Weeds
24 Another parable put he forth unto them, saying, The kingdom of heaven is likened unto a man which sowed good seed in his field: **25** But while men slept, his enemy came and sowed tares among the wheat, and went his way. **26** But when the blade was sprung up, and brought

forth fruit, then appeared the tares also. **27** So the servants of the householder came and said unto him, Sir, didst not thou sow good seed in thy field? from whence then hath it tares? **28** He said unto them, An enemy hath done this. The servants said unto him, Wilt thou then that we go and gather them up? **29** But he said, Nay; lest while ye gather up the tares, ye root up also the wheat with them. **30** Let both grow together until the harvest: and in the time of harvest I will say to the reapers, Gather ye together first the tares, and bind them in bundles to burn them: but gather the wheat into my barn.

The Parable of the Mustard Seed and the Leaven

31 Another parable put he forth unto them, saying, The kingdom of heaven is like to a grain of mustard seed, which a man took, and sowed in his field: **32** Which indeed is the least of all seeds: but when it is grown, it is the greatest among herbs, and becometh a tree, so that the birds of the air come and lodge in the branches thereof. **33** Another parable spake he unto them; The kingdom of heaven is like unto leaven, which a woman took, and hid in three measures of meal, till the whole was leavened.

Explanation for the Disciples

37 He answered and said unto them, He that soweth the good seed is the Son of man; **38** The field is the world; the good seed are the children of the kingdom; but the tares are the children of the wicked one; **39** The enemy that sowed them is the devil; the harvest is the end of the world; and the reapers are the angels. **40** As therefore the tares are gathered and burned in the fire; so shall it be in the end of this world. **41** The Son of man shall send forth his angels, and they shall gather out of his kingdom all things that offend, and them which do iniquity; **42** And shall cast them into a furnace of fire: there shall be wailing and gnashing of teeth. **43** Then shall the righteous shine forth as the sun in the kingdom of their Father. Who hath ears to hear, let him hear.

Parables on the Kingdom of Heaven

44 Again, the kingdom of heaven is like unto treasure hid in a field; the which when a man hath found, he hideth, and for joy thereof goeth and selleth all that he hath, and buyeth that field. **45** Again, the kingdom of heaven is like unto a merchant man, seeking goodly pearls: **46** Who, when he had found one pearl of great price, went and sold all that he had, and bought it. **47** Again, the kingdom of heaven is like unto a net, that was cast into the sea, and gathered of every kind: **48** Which, when it was full, they drew to shore, and sat down, and gathered the good into vessels, but cast the bad away. **49** So shall it be at the end of the world: the angels shall come forth, and sever the wicked from among the just, **50** And shall cast them into the furnace of fire: there shall be wailing and gnashing of teeth. **51** Jesus saith unto them, Have ye understood all these things? They say unto him, Yea, Lord. **52** Then said he unto them, Therefore every scribe *which is* instructed unto the kingdom of heaven is like unto a man *that is* an householder, which bringeth forth out of his treasure *things* new and old.

Without Honour in His own Country

57...But Jesus said unto them, A prophet is not without honour, save in his own country, and in his own house. **58** And he did not many mighty works there because of their unbelief.

Matthew 14

Five Thousand Fed

16 But Jesus said unto them, They need not depart; give ye them to eat. **17** And they say unto him, We have here but five loaves, and two fishes. **18** He said, Bring them hither to me.

Jesus Walks on the Sea

26 And when the disciples saw him walking on the sea, they were troubled, saying, It is a spirit; and they cried out for fear. **27** But straightway Jesus spake unto them, saying, Be of good cheer; it is I; be not afraid. **28** And Peter answered him and said, Lord, if it be thou, bid me come unto thee on the water. **29** And he said, Come. And when Peter was come down out of the ship, he walked on the water, to go to Jesus. **30** But when he saw the wind boisterous, he was afraid; and beginning to sink, he cried, saying, Lord, save me. **31** And immediately Jesus stretched forth *his* hand, and caught him, and said unto him, O thou of little faith, wherefore didst thou doubt?

Matthew 15

Defilement Comes from Within

3 But he answered and said unto them, Why do ye also transgress the commandment of God by your tradition? **4** For God commanded, saying, **Honour thy father and mother:** and, **He that curseth father or mother, let him die the death. 5** But ye say, Whosoever shall say to *his* father or *his* mother, *It is* a gift, by whatsoever thou mightest be profited by me; **6** And honour not his father or his mother, *he shall be free*. Thus have ye made the commandment of God of none effect by your tradition. **7** *Ye* hypocrites, well did Esaias prophesy of you, saying, **8 This people draweth nigh unto me with their mouth, and honoureth me with *their* lips; but their heart is far from me. 9 But in vain they do worship me, teaching *for* doctrines the commandments of men.**

10 And he called the multitude, and said unto them, Hear, and understand: **11** Not that which goeth into the mouth defileth a man; but that which cometh out of the mouth, this defileth a man. **12** Then came his disciples, and said unto him, Knowest thou that the Pharisees were offended, after they heard this saying? **13** But he answered and said, Every plant, which my heavenly Father hath not planted, shall be rooted up. **14** Let them alone: they be blind leaders of the blind. And if the blind lead the blind, both shall fall into the ditch. **15** Then answered Peter and said unto him, Declare unto us this parable. **16** And Jesus said, Are ye also yet without understanding? **17** Do not ye yet understand, that whatsoever entereth in at the mouth goeth into the belly, and is cast out into the draught? **18** But those things which proceed out of the mouth come forth from the heart; and they defile the man. **19** For out of the heart proceed evil thoughts, murders, adulteries, fornications, thefts, false witness, blasphemies: **20** These are *the things* which defile a man: but to eat with unwashen hands defileth not a man.

A Canaanite Woman's Faith
24 But he answered and said, I am not sent but unto the lost sheep of the house of Israel. **25** Then came she and worshipped him, saying, Lord, help me. **26** But he answered and said, It is not meet to take the children's bread, and to cast *it* to dogs. **27** And she said, Truth, Lord: yet the dogs eat of the crumbs which fall from their masters' table. **28** Then Jesus answered and said unto her, O woman, great *is* thy faith: be it unto thee even as thou wilt. And her daughter was made whole from that very hour.

Four Thousand Fed
32 Then Jesus called his disciples unto him, and said, I have compassion on the multitude, because they continue with me now three days, and have nothing to eat: and I will not send them away fasting, lest they faint in the way. **33** And his disciples say unto him, Whence should we have so much bread in the wilderness, as to fill so great a multitude? **34** And Jesus saith unto them, How many loaves have ye? And they said, Seven, and a few little fishes.

Matthew 16

The Demand for a Sign

2 He answered and said unto them, When it is evening, ye say, *It will be* fair weather: for the sky is red. **3** And in the morning, *It will be* foul weather to day: for the sky is red and lowring. O *ye* hypocrites, ye can discern the face of the sky; but can ye not *discern* the signs of the times? **4** A wicked and adulterous generation seeketh after a sign; and there shall no sign be given unto it, but the sign of the prophet Jonas. And he left them, and departed.

The Pharisees and Sadducees' Leaven

5 And when his disciples were come to the other side, they had forgotten to take bread. **6** Then Jesus said unto them, Take heed and beware of the leaven of the Pharisees and of the Sadducees. **7** And they reasoned among themselves, saying, *It is* because we have taken no bread. **8** Which when Jesus perceived, he said unto them, O ye of little faith, why reason ye among yourselves, because ye have brought no bread? **9** Do ye not yet understand, neither remember the five loaves of the five thousand, and how many baskets ye took up? **10** Neither the seven loaves of the four thousand, and how many baskets ye took up? **11** How is it that ye do not understand that I spake it not to you concerning bread, that ye should beware of the leaven of the Pharisees and of the Sadducees?

The Confession of Simon Peter

13 When Jesus came into the coasts of Caesarea Philippi, he asked his disciples, saying, Whom do men say that I the Son of man am? **14** And they said, Some say that thou art John the Baptist: some, Elias; and others, Jeremias, or one of the prophets. **15** He saith unto them, But whom say ye that I am? **16** And Simon Peter answered and said, Thou art the Christ, the Son of the living God. **17** And Jesus answered and said unto him, Blessed art thou, Simon Barjona: for flesh and blood hath not revealed *it* unto thee, but my Father which is in heaven. **18** And I say also unto thee, That thou art Peter, and upon this rock I will build my church; and the gates of hell shall not prevail against it. **19** And I will give unto thee the keys of the kingdom of heaven: and whatsoever thou shalt bind on earth shall be bound in heaven: and whatsoever thou shalt loose on earth shall be loosed in heaven. **20** Then charged he his disciples that they should tell no man that he was Jesus the Christ.

Jesus Prepares His Disciples

21 From that time forth began Jesus to shew unto his disciples, how that he must go unto Jerusalem, and suffer many things of the elders and chief priests and scribes, and be killed, and be raised again the third day. **22** Then Peter took him, and began to rebuke him, saying, Be it far from thee, Lord: this shall not be unto thee. **23** But he turned, and said unto Peter, Get thee behind me, Satan: thou art an offence unto me: for thou savourest not the things that be of God, but those that be of men.

24 Then said Jesus unto his disciples, If any *man* will come after me, let him deny himself, and take up his cross, and follow me. **25** For whosoever will save his life shall lose it: and whosoever will lose his life for my sake shall find it. **26** For what is a man profited, if he shall gain the whole world, and lose his own soul? or what shall a man give in exchange for his soul? **27** For the Son of man shall come in the glory of his Father with his angels; and then he shall reward every man according to his works. **28** Verily I say unto you, There be some standing here, which shall not taste of death, till they see the Son of man coming in his kingdom.

Matthew 17

The Transfiguration

7 And Jesus came and touched them, and said, Arise, and be not afraid. **8** And when they had lifted up their eyes, they saw no man, save Jesus only. **9** And as they came down from the mountain, Jesus charged them, saying, Tell the vision to no man, until the Son of man be risen again from the dead. **10** And his disciples asked him, saying, Why then say the scribes that Elias must first come? **11** And Jesus answered and said unto them, Elias truly shall first come, and restore all things. **12** But I say unto you, That Elias is come already, and they knew him not, but have done unto him whatsoever they listed. Likewise shall also the Son of man suffer of them.

The Healing of a Devil-Possessed Boy

15 Lord, have mercy on my son: for he is lunatick, and sore vexed: for ofttimes he falleth into the fire, and oft into the water. **16** And I brought him to thy disciples, and they could not cure him. **17** Then Jesus answered and said, O faithless and perverse generation, how long shall I be with you? how long shall I suffer you? bring him hither to me. **18** And Jesus rebuked the devil; and he departed out of him: and the child was cured from that very hour. **19** Then came the disciples to Jesus apart, and said, Why could not we cast him out? **20** And Jesus said unto them, Because of your unbelief: for verily I say unto you, If ye have faith as a grain of mustard seed, ye shall say unto this mountain, Remove hence to yonder place; and it shall remove; and nothing shall be impossible unto you. **21** Howbeit this kind goeth not out but by prayer and fasting. **22** And while they abode in Galilee, Jesus said unto them, The Son of man shall be betrayed into the hands of men: **23** And they shall kill him, and the third day he shall be raised again. And they were exceeding sorry.

The Question of Paying Tribute

24 And when they were come to Capernaum, they that received tribute money came to Peter, and said, Doth not your master pay tribute? **25** He saith, Yes. And when he was come into the house, Jesus prevented him, saying, What thinkest thou, Simon? of whom do the kings of the earth take custom or tribute? of their own children, or of strangers? **26** Peter saith unto him, Of strangers. Jesus saith unto him, Then are the children free. **27** Notwithstanding, lest we should offend them, go thou to the sea, and cast an hook, and take up the fish that first cometh up; and when thou hast opened his mouth, thou shalt find a piece of money: that take, and give unto them for me and thee.

Matthew 18

The Least is the Greatest

2 And Jesus called a little child unto him, and set him in the midst of them, **3** And said, Verily I say unto you, Except ye be converted, and become as little children, ye shall not enter into the kingdom of heaven. **4** Whosoever therefore shall humble himself as this little child, the same is greatest in the kingdom of heaven. **5** And whoso shall receive one such little child in my name receiveth me. **6** But whoso shall offend one of these little ones which believe in me, it were better for him that a millstone were hanged about his neck, and *that* he were drowned in the depth of the sea.

7 Woe unto the world because of offences! for it must needs be that offences come; but woe to that man by whom the offence cometh! **8** Wherefore if thy hand or thy foot offend thee, cut them off, and cast *them* from thee: it is better for thee to enter into life halt or maimed, rather than having two hands or two feet to be cast into everlasting fire. **9** And if thine eye offend thee, pluck it out, and cast *it* from thee: it is better for thee to enter into life with one eye, rather than having two eyes to be cast into hell fire. **10** Take heed that ye despise not one of these little ones; for I say unto you, That in heaven their angels do always behold the face of my Father which is in heaven. **11** For the Son of man is come to save that which was lost.

The Parable of the Lost Sheep

12 How think ye? if a man have an hundred sheep, and one of them be gone astray, doth he not leave the ninety and nine, and goeth into the mountains, and seeketh that which is gone astray? **13** And if so be that he find it, verily I say unto you, he rejoiceth more of that *sheep*, than of the ninety and nine which went not astray. **14** Even so it is not the will of your Father which is in heaven, that one of these little ones should perish.

Restoring Christian Relationships

15 Moreover if thy brother shall trespass against thee, go and tell him his fault between thee and him alone: if he shall hear thee, thou hast gained thy brother. **16** But if he will not hear *thee, then* take with thee one or two more, **that in the mouth of two or three witnesses every word may be established.** **17** And if he shall neglect to hear them, tell *it* unto the church: but if he neglect to hear the church, let him be unto thee as an heathen man and a publican. **18** Verily I say unto you, Whatsoever ye shall bind on earth shall be bound in heaven: and whatsoever ye shall loose on earth shall be loosed in heaven. **19** Again I say unto you, That if two of you shall agree on earth as touching any thing that they shall ask, it shall be done for them of my Father which is in heaven. **20** For where two or three are gathered together in my name, there am I in the midst of them.

21 Then came Peter to him, and said, Lord, how oft shall my brother sin against me, and I forgive him? till seven times? **22** Jesus saith unto him, I say not unto thee, Until seven times: but, Until seventy times seven.

The Unforgiving Servant

23 Therefore is the kingdom of heaven likened unto a certain king, which would take account of his servants. **24** And when he had begun to reckon, one was brought unto him, which owed him ten thousand talents. **25** But forasmuch as he had not to pay, his lord commanded him to be sold, and his wife, and children, and all that he had, and payment to be made. **26** The servant therefore fell down, and worshipped him, saying, Lord, have patience with me, and I will pay thee all. **27** Then the lord of that servant was moved with compassion, and loosed him, and forgave him the debt. **28** But the same servant went out, and found one of his fellowservants, which owed him an hundred pence: and he laid hands on him, and took *him* by the throat, saying, Pay me that thou owest. **29** And his fellowservant fell down at his feet, and besought him, saying, Have patience with me, and I will pay thee all. **30** And he would not: but went and cast him into prison, till he should pay the debt. **31** So when his fellowservants saw what was done, they were very sorry, and came and told unto their lord all that was done. **32** Then his lord, after that he had called him, said unto him, O thou wicked servant, I forgave thee all that debt, because thou desiredst me: **33** Shouldest not thou also have had compassion on thy fellowservant, even as I had pity on thee? **34** And his lord was wroth, and delivered him to the tormentors, till he should pay all that was due unto him. **35** So likewise shall my heavenly Father do also unto you, if ye from your hearts forgive not every one his brother their trespasses.

Matthew 19

Teachings on Divorce

3 The Pharisees also came unto him, tempting him, and saying unto him, Is it lawful for a man to put away his wife for every cause? **4** And he answered and said unto them, Have ye not read, that he which made *them* at the beginning made them male and female, **5** And said, **For this cause shall a man leave father and mother, and shall cleave to his wife: and they twain shall be one flesh?** **6** Wherefore they are no more twain, but one flesh. What therefore God hath joined together, let not man put asunder. **7** They say unto him, Why did Moses then command to give a writing of divorcement, and to put her away? **8** He saith unto them, Moses because of the hardness of your hearts suffered you to put away your wives: but from the beginning it was not so. **9** And I say unto you, Whosoever shall put away his wife, except *it be* for fornication, and shall marry another, committeth adultery: and whoso marrieth her which is put away doth commit adultery. **10** His disciples say unto him, If the case of the man be so with his wife, it is not good to marry. **11** But he said unto them, All *men* cannot receive this saying, save *they* to whom it is given. **12** For there are some eunuchs, which were so born from *their* mother's womb: and there are some eunuchs, which were made eunuchs of men: and there be eunuchs, which have made themselves eunuchs for the kingdom of heaven's sake. He that is able to receive *it*, let him receive *it*.

Jesus and Little Children

14 But Jesus said, Suffer little children, and forbid them not, to come unto me: for of such is the kingdom of heaven.

The Rich Young Man

16 And, behold, one came and said unto him, Good Master, what good thing shall I do, that I may have eternal life? **17** And he said unto him, Why callest thou me good? *there is* none good but one, *that is*, God: but if thou wilt enter into life, keep the commandments. **18** He saith unto him, Which? Jesus said, Thou shalt do no murder, Thou shalt not commit adultery, Thou shalt not steal, Thou shalt not bear false witness, **19** Honour thy father and *thy* mother: and, Thou shalt love thy neighbour as thyself. **20** The young man saith unto him, All these things have I kept from my youth up: what lack I yet? **21** Jesus said unto him, If thou wilt be perfect, go *and* sell that thou hast, and give to the poor, and thou shalt have treasure in heaven: and come *and* follow me. **22** But when the young man heard that saying, he went away sorrowful: for he had great possessions.

23 Then said Jesus unto his disciples, Verily I say unto you, That a rich man shall hardly enter into the kingdom of heaven. **24** And again I say unto you, It is easier for a camel to go through the eye of a needle, than for a rich man to enter into the kingdom of God. **25** When his disciples heard it, they were exceedingly amazed, saying, Who then can be saved? **26** But Jesus beheld them, and said unto them, With men this is impossible; but with God all things are possible. **27** Then answered Peter and said unto him, Behold, we have forsaken all, and followed thee; what shall we have therefore? **28** And Jesus said unto them, Verily I say unto you, That ye which have followed me, in the regeneration when the Son of man shall sit in the throne of his glory, ye also shall sit upon twelve thrones, judging the twelve tribes of Israel. **29** And every one that hath forsaken houses, or brethren, or sisters, or father, or mother, or wife, or children, or lands, for my name's sake, shall receive an hundredfold, and shall inherit everlasting life. **30** But many that are first shall be last; and the last shall be first.

Matthew 20

The Parable of the Hired Labourers

1 For the kingdom of heaven is like unto a man *that is* an householder, which went out early in the morning to hire labourers into his vineyard. **2** And when he had agreed with the labourers for a penny a day, he sent them into his vineyard. **3** And he went out about the third hour, and saw others standing idle in the marketplace, **4** And said unto them; Go ye also into the vineyard, and whatsoever is right I will give you. And they went their way. **5** Again he went out about the sixth and ninth hour, and did likewise. **6** And about the eleventh hour he went out, and found others standing idle, and saith unto them, Why stand ye here all the day idle? **7** They say unto him, Because no man hath hired us. He saith unto them, Go ye also into the vineyard; and whatsoever is right, *that* shall ye receive. **8** So when even was come, the lord of the vineyard saith unto his steward, Call the labourers, and give them *their* hire, beginning from the last unto the first. **9** And when they came that *were hired* about the eleventh hour, they received every man a penny. **10** But when the first came, they supposed that they should have received more; and they likewise received every man a penny. **11** And when they had received *it*, they murmured against the goodman of the house, **12** Saying, These last have wrought *but* one hour, and thou hast made them equal unto us, which have borne the burden and heat of the day. **13** But he answered one of them, and said, Friend, I do thee no wrong: didst not thou agree with me for a penny? **14** Take *that* thine *is*, and go thy way: I will give unto this last, even as unto thee. **15** Is it not lawful for me to do what I will with mine own? Is thine eye evil, because I am good? **16** So the last shall be first, and the first last: for many be called, but few chosen.

Prediction of Jesus' Death and Resurrection

18 Behold, we go up to Jerusalem; and the Son of man shall be betrayed unto the chief priests and unto the scribes, and they shall condemn him to death, **19** And shall deliver him to the Gentiles to mock, and to scourge, and to crucify *him*: and the third day he shall rise again.

A Request for James and John

20 Then came to him the mother of Zebedee's children with her sons, worshipping *him*, and desiring a certain thing of him. **21** And he said unto her, What wilt thou? She saith unto him, Grant that these my two sons may sit, the one on thy right hand, and the other on the left, in thy kingdom. **22** But Jesus answered and said, Ye know not what ye ask. Are ye able to drink of the cup that I shall drink of, and to be baptized with the baptism that I am baptized with? They say unto him, We are able. **23** And he saith unto them, Ye shall drink indeed of my cup, and be baptized with the baptism that I am baptized with: but to sit on my right hand, and on my left, is not mine to give, but *it shall be given to them* for whom it is prepared of my Father. **24** And when the ten heard *it*, they were moved with indignation against the two brethren. **25** But Jesus called them *unto him*, and said, Ye know that the princes of the Gentiles exercise dominion over them, and they that are great exercise authority upon them. **26** But it shall not be so among you: but whosoever will be great among you, let him be your minister; **27** And whosoever will be chief among you, let him be your servant: **28** Even as the Son of man came not to be ministered unto, but to minister, and to give his life a ransom for many.

Jesus Healed Two Blind Men
32 And Jesus stood still, and called them, and said, What will ye that I shall do unto you? **33** They say unto him, Lord, that our eyes may be opened. **34** So Jesus had compassion *on them*, and touched their eyes: and immediately their eyes received sight, and they followed him.

Matthew 21
The Triumphal Entry
1 And when they drew nigh unto Jerusalem, and were come to Bethphage, unto the mount of Olives, then sent Jesus two disciples, **2** Saying unto them, Go into the village over against you, and straightway ye shall find an ass tied, and a colt with her: loose *them*, and bring *them* unto me. **3** And if any *man* say ought unto you, ye shall say, The Lord hath need of them; and straightway he will send them.

Cleansing the Temple
13 And said unto them, It is written, **My house shall be called the house of prayer;** but ye have made it a den of thieves. **14** And the blind and the lame came to him in the temple; and he healed them. **15** And when the chief priests and scribes saw the wonderful things that he did, and the children crying in the temple, and saying, Hosanna to the Son of David; they were sore displeased, **16** And said unto him, Hearest thou what these say? And Jesus saith unto them, Yea; have ye never read, **Out of the mouth of babes and sucklings thou hast perfected praise?**

The Withered Fig Tree

18 Now in the morning as he returned into the city, he hungered. **19** And when he saw a fig tree in the way, he came to it, and found nothing thereon, but leaves only, and said unto it, Let no fruit grow on thee henceforward for ever. And presently the fig tree withered away. **20** And when the disciples saw *it*, they marvelled, saying, How soon is the fig tree withered away! **21** Jesus answered and said unto them, Verily I say unto you, If ye have faith, and doubt not, ye shall not only do this *which is done* to the fig tree, but also if ye shall say unto this mountain, Be thou removed, and be thou cast into the sea; it shall be done. **22** And all things, whatsoever ye shall ask in prayer, believing, ye shall receive.

The Authority of Jesus

24 And Jesus answered and said unto them, I also will ask you one thing, which if ye tell me, I in like wise will tell you by what authority I do these things. **25** The baptism of John, whence was it? from heaven, or of men? And they reasoned with themselves, saying, If we shall say, From heaven; he will say unto us, Why did ye not then believe him? **26** But if we shall say, Of men; we fear the people; for all hold John as a prophet. **27** And they answered Jesus, and said, We cannot tell. And he said unto them, Neither tell I you by what authority I do these things.

The Parable of Two Sons

28 But what think ye? A *certain* man had two sons; and he came to the first, and said, Son, go work to day in my vineyard. **29** He answered and said, I will not: but afterward he repented, and went. **30** And he came to the second, and said likewise. And he answered and said, I *go*, sir: and went not. **31** Whether of them twain did the will of *his* father? They say unto him, The first. Jesus saith unto them, Verily I say unto you, That the publicans and the harlots go into the kingdom of God before you. **32** For John came unto you in the way of righteousness, and ye believed him not: but the publicans and the harlots believed him: and ye, when ye had seen *it*, repented not afterward, that ye might believe him.

The Parable of the Vineyard

33 Hear another parable: There was a certain householder, which planted a vineyard, and hedged it round about, and digged a winepress in it, and built a tower, and let it out to husbandmen, and went into a far country: **34** And when the time of the fruit drew near, he sent his servants to the husbandmen, that they might receive the fruits of it. **35** And the husbandmen took his servants, and beat one, and killed another, and stoned another. **36** Again, he sent other servants more than the first: and they did unto them likewise. **37** But last of all he sent unto them his son, saying, They will reverence my son. **38** But when the husbandmen saw the son, they said among themselves, This is the heir; come, let us kill him, and let us seize on his inheritance. **39** And they caught him, and cast *him* out of the vineyard, and slew *him*. **40** When the lord therefore of the vineyard cometh, what will he do unto those husbandmen? **41** They say unto him, He will miserably destroy those wicked men, and will let out *his* vineyard unto other husbandmen, which shall render him the fruits in their seasons. **42** Jesus saith unto them, Did ye never read in the scriptures, **The stone which the builders rejected, the same is become the head of the corner: this is the Lord's doing, and it is marvellous in our eyes?** **43** Therefore say I unto you, The kingdom of God shall be taken from you, and given to a nation bringing forth the fruits thereof. **44** And whosoever shall fall on this stone shall be broken: but on whomsoever it shall fall, it will grind him to powder.

Matthew 22

The Parable of the Wedding Banquet

1 And Jesus answered and spake unto them again by parables, and said, **2** The kingdom of heaven is like unto a certain king, which made a marriage for his son, **3** And sent forth his servants to call them that were bidden to the wedding: and they would not come. **4** Again, he sent forth other servants, saying, Tell them which are bidden, Behold, I have prepared my dinner: my oxen and *my* fatlings *are* killed, and all things *are* ready: come unto the marriage. **5** But they made light of *it*, and went their ways, one to his farm, another to his merchandise: **6** And the remnant took his servants, and entreated *them* spitefully, and slew *them*. **7** But when the king heard *thereof*, he was wroth: and he sent forth his armies, and destroyed those murderers, and burned up their city. **8** Then saith he to his servants, The wedding is ready, but they which were bidden were not worthy. **9** Go ye therefore into the highways, and as many as ye shall find, bid to the marriage. **10** So those servants went out into the highways, and gathered together all as many as they found, both bad and good: and the wedding was furnished with guests. **11** And when the king came in to see the guests, he saw there a man which had not on a wedding garment: **12** And he saith unto him, Friend, how camest thou in hither not having a wedding garment? And he was speechless. **13** Then said the king to the servants, Bind him hand and foot, and take him away, and cast *him* into outer darkness; there shall be weeping and gnashing of teeth. **14** For many are called, but few *are* chosen.

Paying Tribute to Caesar and to God

17 Tell us therefore, What thinkest thou? Is it lawful to give tribute unto Caesar, or not? **18** But Jesus perceived their wickedness, and said, Why tempt ye me, *ye* hypocrites? **19** Shew me the tribute money. And they brought unto him a penny. **20** And he saith unto them, Whose *is* this image and superscription? **21** They say unto him, Caesar's. Then saith he unto them, Render therefore unto Caesar the things which are Caesar's; and unto God the things that are God's.

Teachings on the Resurrection

29 Jesus answered and said unto them, Ye do err, not knowing the scriptures, nor the power of God. 30 For in the resurrection they neither marry, nor are given in marriage, but are as the angels of God in heaven. 31 But as touching the resurrection of the dead, have ye not read that which was spoken unto you by God, saying, 32 **I am the God of Abraham, and the God of Isaac, and the God of Jacob?** God is not the God of the dead, but of the living.

The Greatest Commandment

35 Then one of them, which was a lawyer, asked him a question, tempting him, and saying, 36 Master, which is the great commandment in the law? 37 Jesus said unto him, **Thou shalt love the Lord thy God with all thy heart, and with all thy soul, and with all thy mind.** 38 This is the first and great commandment. 39 And the second *is* like unto it, **Thou shalt love thy neighbour as thyself.** 40 On these two commandments hang all the law and the prophets.

Pharisees Questioned

41 While the Pharisees were gathered together, Jesus asked them, 42 Saying, What think ye of Christ? whose son is he? They say unto him, The Son of David. 43 He saith unto them, How then doth David in spirit call him Lord, saying, 44 **The LORD said unto my Lord, Sit thou on my right hand, till I make thine enemies thy footstool?** 45 If David then call him Lord, how is he his son?

Matthew 23

The Scribes and Pharisees

1 Then spake Jesus to the multitude, and to his disciples, 2 Saying, The scribes and the Pharisees sit in Moses' seat: 3 All therefore whatsoever they bid you observe, *that* observe and do; but do not ye after their works: for they say, and do not. 4 For they bind heavy burdens and

grievous to be borne, and lay *them* on men's shoulders; but they *themselves* will not move them with one of their fingers.

Hypocrisy Denounced

5 But all their works they do for to be seen of men: they make broad their phylacteries, and enlarge the borders of their garments, 6 And love the uppermost rooms at feasts, and the chief seats in the synagogues, 7 And greetings in the markets, and to be called of men, Rabbi, Rabbi. 8 But be not ye called Rabbi: for one is your Master, *even* Christ; and all ye are brethren. 9 And call no *man* your father upon the earth: for one is your Father, which is in heaven. 10 Neither be ye called masters: for one is your Master, *even* Christ. 11 But he that is greatest among you shall be your servant. 12 And whosoever shall exalt himself shall be abased; and he that shall humble himself shall be exalted.

13 But woe unto you, scribes and Pharisees, hypocrites! for ye shut up the kingdom of heaven against men: for ye neither go in *yourselves*, neither suffer ye them that are entering to go in. 14 Woe unto you, scribes and Pharisees, hypocrites! for ye devour widows' houses, and for a pretence make long prayer: therefore ye shall receive the greater damnation. 15 Woe unto you, scribes and Pharisees, hypocrites! for ye compass sea and land to make one proselyte, and when he is made, ye make him twofold more the child of hell than yourselves.

Woe on Scribes and Pharisees

16 Woe unto you, *ye* blind guides, which say, Whosoever shall swear by the temple, it is nothing; but whosoever shall swear by the gold of the temple, he is a debtor! 17 *Ye* fools and blind: for whether is greater, the gold, or the temple that sanctifieth the gold? 18 And, Whosoever shall swear by the altar, it is nothing; but whosoever sweareth by the gift that is upon it, he is guilty. 19 *Ye* fools and blind: for whether *is* greater, the gift, or the altar that sanctifieth the gift? 20 Whoso therefore shall swear by the

altar, sweareth by it, and by all things thereon. 21 And whoso shall swear by the temple, sweareth by it, and by him that dwelleth therein. 22 And he that shall swear by heaven, sweareth by the throne of God, and by him that sitteth thereon. 23 Woe unto you, scribes and Pharisees, hypocrites! for ye pay tithe of mint and anise and cummin, and have omitted the weightier *matters* of the law, judgment, mercy, and faith: these ought ye to have done, and not to leave the other undone. 24 *Ye* blind guides, which strain at a gnat, and swallow a camel. 25 Woe unto you, scribes and Pharisees, hypocrites! for ye make clean the outside of the cup and of the platter, but within they are full of extortion and excess. 26 *Thou* blind Pharisee, cleanse first that *which is* within the cup and platter, that the outside of them may be clean also. 27 Woe unto you, scribes and Pharisees, hypocrites! for ye are like unto whited sepulchres, which indeed appear beautiful outward, but are within full of dead *men's* bones, and of all uncleanness. 28 Even so ye also outwardly appear righteous unto men, but within ye are full of hypocrisy and iniquity. 29 Woe unto you, scribes and Pharisees, hypocrites! because ye build the tombs of the prophets, and garnish the sepulchres of the righteous, 30 And say, If we had been in the days of our fathers, we would not have been partakers with them in the blood of the prophets. 31 Wherefore ye be witnesses unto yourselves, that ye are the children of them which killed the prophets. 32 Fill ye up then the measure of your fathers. 33 *Ye* serpents, *ye* generation of vipers, how can ye escape the damnation of hell?

34 Wherefore, behold, I send unto you prophets, and wise men, and scribes: and *some* of them ye shall kill and crucify; and *some* of them shall ye scourge in your synagogues, and persecute *them* from city to city: 35 That upon you may come all the righteous blood shed upon the earth, from the blood of righteous Abel unto the blood of Zacharias son of Barachias, whom ye slew between the temple and the altar. 36 Verily I say unto you, All these things shall come upon this generation.

Judgment on Israel

37 O Jerusalem, Jerusalem, *thou* that killest the prophets, and stonest them which are sent unto thee, how often would I have gathered thy children together, even as a hen gathereth her chickens under *her* wings, and ye would not! **38** Behold, your house is left unto you desolate. **39** For I say unto you, Ye shall not see me henceforth, till ye shall say, Blessed *is* he that cometh in the name of the Lord.

Matthew 24

Signs of the End of the Age

1 And Jesus went out, and departed from the temple: and his disciples came to *him* for to shew him the buildings of the temple. **2** And Jesus said unto them, See ye not all these things? verily I say unto you, There shall not be left here one stone upon another, that shall not be thrown down. **3** And as he sat upon the mount of Olives, the disciples came unto him privately, saying, Tell us, when shall these things be? and what *shall be* the sign of thy coming, and of the end of the world?

4 And Jesus answered and said unto them, Take heed that no man deceive you. **5** For many shall come in my name, saying, I am Christ; and shall deceive many. **6** And ye shall hear of wars and rumours of wars: see that ye be not troubled: for all *these things* must come to pass, but the end is not yet. **7** For nation shall rise against nation, and kingdom against kingdom: and there shall be famines, and pestilences, and earthquakes, in divers places. **8** All these *are* the beginning of sorrows. **9** Then shall they deliver you up to be afflicted, and shall kill you: and ye shall be hated of all nations for my name's sake. **10** And then shall many be offended, and shall betray one another, and shall hate one another. **11** And many false prophets shall rise, and shall deceive many. **12** And because iniquity shall abound, the love of many shall wax cold. **13** But he that shall endure unto the end, the same shall be saved. **14** And this gospel of the kingdom shall be preached in all the world for a witness unto all nations; and then shall the end come.

The Coming of the Son of Man

15 When ye therefore shall see the abomination of desolation, spoken of by Daniel the prophet, stand in the holy place, (whoso readeth, let him understand:) **16** Then let them which be in Judaea flee into the mountains: **17** Let him which is on the housetop not come down to take any thing out of his house: **18** Neither let him which is in the field return back to take his clothes. **19** And woe unto them that are with child, and to them that give suck in those days! **20** But pray ye that your flight be not in the winter, neither on the sabbath day: **21** For then shall be great tribulation, such as was not since the beginning of the world to this time, no, nor ever shall be. **22** And except those days should be shortened, there should no flesh be saved: but for the elect's sake those days shall be shortened. **23** Then if any man shall say unto you, Lo, here *is* Christ, or there; believe *it* not. **24** For there shall arise false Christs, and false prophets, and shall shew great signs and wonders; insomuch that, if *it were* possible, they shall deceive the very elect. **25** Behold, I have told you before. **26** Wherefore if they shall say unto you, Behold, he is in the desert; go not forth: behold, *he is* in the secret chambers; believe *it* not. **27** For as the lightning cometh out of the east, and shineth even unto the west; so shall also the coming of the Son of man be. **28** For wheresoever the carcase is, there will the eagles be gathered together. **29** Immediately after the tribulation of those days shall the sun be darkened, and the moon shall not give her light, and the stars shall fall from heaven, and the powers of the heavens shall be shaken: **30** And then shall appear the sign of the Son of man in heaven: and then shall all the tribes of the earth mourn, and they shall see the Son of man coming in the clouds of heaven with power and great glory. **31** And he shall send his angels with a great sound of a trumpet, and they shall gather together his elect from the four winds, from one end of heaven to the other.

The Parable of the Fig Tree

32 Now learn a parable of the fig tree; When his branch is yet tender, and putteth forth leaves, ye know that summer *is* nigh: **33** So likewise ye, when ye shall see all these things, know that it is near, *even* at the doors. **34** Verily I say unto you, This generation shall not pass, till all these things be fulfilled. **35** Heaven and earth shall pass away, but my words shall not pass away.

Be Ready!

36 But of that day and hour knoweth no *man*, no, not the angels of heaven, but my Father only. **37** But as the days of Noe *were*, so shall also the coming of the Son of man be. **38** For as in the days that were before the flood they were eating and drinking, marrying and giving in marriage, until the day that Noe entered into the ark, **39** And knew not until the flood came, and took them all away; so shall also the coming of the Son of man be. **40** Then shall two be in the field; the one shall be taken, and the other left. **41** Two *women shall be* grinding at the mill; the one shall be taken, and the other left. **42** Watch therefore: for ye know not what hour your Lord doth come. **43** But know this, that if the goodman of the house had known in what watch the thief would come, he would have watched, and would not have suffered his house to be broken up. **44** Therefore be ye also ready: for in such an hour as ye think not the Son of man cometh.

The Faithful and Wise Slave

45 Who then is a faithful and wise servant, whom his lord hath made ruler over his household, to give them meat in due season? **46** Blessed *is* that servant, whom his lord when he cometh shall find so doing. **47** Verily I say unto you, That he shall make him ruler over all his goods. **48** But and if that evil servant shall say in his heart, My lord delayeth his coming; **49** And shall begin to smite *his* fellowservants, and to eat and drink with the drunken; **50** The lord of that servant shall come in a day when he looketh not for *him*, and in an hour that he is not aware of, **51** And shall cut him asunder, and appoint *him* his portion with the hypocrites: there shall be weeping and gnashing of teeth.

Matthew 25

The Parable of the Ten Virgins

1 Then shall the kingdom of heaven be likened unto ten virgins, which took their lamps, and went forth to meet the bridegroom. **2** And five of them were wise, and five *were* foolish. **3** They that *were* foolish took their lamps, and took no oil with them: **4** But the wise took oil in their vessels with their lamps. **5** While the bridegroom tarried, they all slumbered and slept. **6** And at midnight there was a cry made, Behold, the bridegroom cometh; go ye out to meet him. **7** Then all those virgins arose, and trimmed their lamps. **8** And the foolish said unto the wise, Give us of your oil; for our lamps are gone out. **9** But the wise answered, saying, *Not so*; lest there be not enough for us and you: but go ye rather to them that sell, and buy for yourselves. **10** And while they went to buy, the bridegroom came; and they that were ready went in with him to the marriage: and the door was shut. **11** Afterward came also the other virgins, saying, Lord, Lord, open to us. **12** But he answered and said, Verily I say unto you, I know you not. **13** Watch therefore, for ye know neither the day nor the hour wherein the Son of man cometh.

The Parable of the Talents

14 For the kingdom of heaven is as a man travelling into a far country, who called his own servants, and delivered unto them his goods. **15** And unto one he gave five talents, to another two, and to another one; to every man according to his several ability; and straightway took his journey. **16** Then he that had received the five talents went and traded with the same, and made them other five talents. **17** And likewise he that had received two, he also gained other two. **18** But he that had received one went and digged in the earth, and hid his lord's money. **19** After a long time the lord of those servants cometh, and reckoneth with them. **20** And so he that had received five talents came and brought other five talents, saying, Lord, thou deliveredst unto me five talents: behold, I have gained beside them five talents more. **21** His lord said unto him, Well done, thou good and faithful servant: thou hast been faithful over a few things, I will make thee ruler over many things: enter thou into the joy of thy lord. **22** He also that had received two talents came and said, Lord, thou deliveredst unto me two talents: behold, I have gained two other talents beside them. **23** His lord said unto him, Well done, good and faithful servant; thou hast been faithful over a few things, I will make thee ruler over many things: enter thou into the joy of thy lord. **24** Then he which had received the one talent came and said, Lord, I knew thee that thou art an hard man, reaping where thou hast not sown, and gathering where thou hast not strawed: **25** And I was afraid, and went and hid thy talent in the earth: lo, there thou hast that is thine. **26** His lord answered and said unto him, Thou wicked and slothful servant, thou knewest that I reap where I sowed not, and gather where I have not strawed: **27** Thou oughtest therefore to have put my money to the exchangers, and then at my coming I should have received mine own with usury. **28** Take therefore the talent from him, and give *it* unto him which hath ten talents. **29** For unto every one that hath shall be given, and he shall have abundance: but from him that hath not shall be taken away even that which he hath. **30** And cast ye the unprofitable servant into outer darkness: there shall be weeping and gnashing of teeth.

The Judgment: Separation of Sheep and Goats
31 When the Son of man shall come in his glory, and all the holy angels with him, then shall he sit upon the throne of his glory: **32** And before him shall be gathered

all nations: and he shall separate them one from another, as a shepherd divideth his sheep from the goats: **33** And he shall set the sheep on his right hand, but the goats on the left. **34** Then shall the King say unto them on his right hand, Come, ye blessed of my Father, inherit the kingdom prepared for you from the foundation of the world: **35** For I was an hungred, and ye gave me meat: I was thirsty, and ye gave me drink: I was a stranger, and ye took me in: **36** Naked, and ye clothed me: I was sick, and ye visited me: I was in prison, and ye came unto me. **37** Then shall the righteous answer him, saying, Lord, when saw we thee an hungred, and fed thee? or thirsty, and gave thee drink? **38** When saw we thee a stranger, and took thee in? or naked, and clothed thee? **39** Or when saw we thee sick, or in prison, and came unto thee? **40** And the King shall answer and say unto them, Verily I say unto you, Inasmuch as ye have done it unto one of the least of these my brethren, ye have done it unto me. **41** Then shall he say also unto them on the left hand, Depart from me, ye cursed, into everlasting fire, prepared for the devil and his angels: **42** For I was an hungred, and ye gave me no meat: I was thirsty, and ye gave me no drink: **43** I was a stranger, and ye took me not in: naked, and ye clothed me not: sick, and in prison, and ye visited me not. **44** Then shall they also answer him, saying, Lord, when saw we thee an hungred, or athirst, or a stranger, or naked, or sick, or in prison, and did not minister unto thee? **45** Then shall he answer them, saying, Verily I say unto you, Inasmuch as ye did it not to one of the least of these, ye did *it* not to me. **46** And these shall go away into everlasting punishment: but the righteous into life eternal.

Matthew 26

The Plot Against Jesus

1 And it came to pass, when Jesus had finished all these sayings, he said unto his disciples, **2** Ye know that after two days is the feast of the passover, and the Son of man is betrayed to be crucified.

Jesus' Anointing

10 When Jesus understood it, he said unto them, Why trouble ye the woman? for she hath wrought a good work upon me. **11** For ye have the poor always with you; but me ye have not always. **12** For in that she hath poured this ointment on my body, she did *it* for my burial. **13** Verily I say unto you, Wheresoever this gospel shall be preached in the whole world, *there* shall also this, that this woman hath done, be told for a memorial of her.

The Passover

17 Now the first day of the feast of unleavened bread the disciples came to Jesus, saying unto him, Where wilt thou that we prepare for thee to eat the passover? **18** And he said, Go into the city to such a man, and say unto him, The Master saith, My time is at hand; I will keep the passover at thy house with my disciples. **19** And the disciples did as Jesus had appointed them; and they made ready the passover. **20** Now when the even was come, he sat down with the twelve. **21** And as they did eat, he said, Verily I say unto you, that one of you shall betray me. **22** And they were exceeding sorrowful, and began every one of them to say unto him, Lord, is it I? **23** And he answered and said, He that dippeth his hand with me in the dish, the same shall betray me. **24** The Son of man goeth as it is written of him: but woe unto that man by whom the Son of man is betrayed! it had been good for that man if he had not been born. **25** Then Judas, which betrayed him, answered and said, Master, is it I? He said unto him, Thou hast said.

The Lord's Supper

26 And as they were eating, Jesus took bread, and blessed *it*, and brake *it*, and gave *it* to the disciples, and said, Take, eat; this is my body. **27** And he took the cup, and gave thanks, and gave *it* to them, saying, Drink ye all of it; **28** For this is my blood of the new testament, which is shed for many for the remission of sins. **29** But I say unto you, I will not drink henceforth of this fruit of the vine, until that day when I drink it new with you in my Father's kingdom. 30 And when they had sung an hymn, they went out into the mount of Olives.

The Prediction of Peter's Denial

31 Then saith Jesus unto them, All ye shall be offended because of me this night: for it is written, **I will smite the shepherd, and the sheep of the flock shall be scattered abroad.** 32 But after I am risen again, I will go before you into Galilee. 33 Peter answered and said unto him, Though all *men* shall be offended because of thee, *yet* will I never be offended. 34 Jesus said unto him, Verily I say unto thee, That this night, before the cock crow, thou shalt deny me thrice.

Gethsemane

36 Then cometh Jesus with them unto a place called Gethsemane, and saith unto the disciples, Sit ye here, while I go and pray yonder. 37 And he took with him Peter and the two sons of Zebedee, and began to be sorrowful and very heavy. 38 Then saith he unto them, My soul is exceeding sorrowful, even unto death: tarry ye here, and watch with me. 39 And he went a little further, and fell on his face, and prayed, saying, O my Father, if it be possible, let this cup pass from me: nevertheless not as I will, but as thou *wilt*. 40 And he cometh unto the disciples, and findeth them asleep, and saith unto Peter, What, could ye not watch with me one hour? 41 Watch and pray, that ye enter not into temptation: the spirit indeed *is* willing, but the flesh *is* weak. 42 He went away again the second time, and prayed, saying, O my Father, if this cup may not pass away from me, except I drink it, thy will be done. 43 And he came and found them asleep again: for their eyes were heavy. 44 And he left them, and went away again, and prayed the third time, saying the same words. 45 Then cometh he to his disciples, and saith unto them, Sleep on now, and take *your* rest: behold, the hour is at hand, and the Son of man is betrayed into the hands of sinners. 46

Rise, let us be going: behold, he is at hand that doth betray me.

Jesus' Betrayal and Arrest

50 And Jesus said unto him, Friend, wherefore art thou come? Then came they, and laid hands on Jesus, and took him. **51** And, behold, one of them which were with Jesus stretched out *his* hand, and drew his sword, and struck a servant of the high priest's, and smote off his ear. **52** Then said Jesus unto him, Put up again thy sword into his place: for all they that take the sword shall perish with the sword. **53** Thinkest thou that I cannot now pray to my Father, and he shall presently give me more than twelve legions of angels? **54** But how then shall the scriptures be fulfilled, that thus it must be? **55** In that same hour said Jesus to the multitudes, Are ye come out as against a thief with swords and staves for to take me? I sat daily with you teaching in the temple, and ye laid no hold on me. **56** But all this was done, that the scriptures of the prophets might be fulfilled. Then all the disciples forsook him, and fled.

Jesus before Caiaphas

64 Jesus saith unto him, Thou hast said: nevertheless I say unto you, Hereafter shall ye see the Son of man sitting on the right hand of power, and coming in the clouds of heaven.

Peter's Denials

75 And Peter remembered the word of Jesus, which said unto him, Before the cock crow, thou shalt deny me thrice. And he went out, and wept bitterly.

Matthew 27

Jesus Appears Before Pilate

11 And Jesus stood before the governor: and the governor asked him, saying, Art thou the King of the Jews? And Jesus said unto him, Thou sayest.

The Crucifixion of Jesus

46 And about the ninth hour Jesus cried with a loud voice, saying, **Eli, Eli, lama sabachthani?** that is to say, **My God, my God, why hast thou forsaken me?**

The Guard at the Tomb

62 Now the next day, that followed the day of the preparation, the chief priests and Pharisees came together unto Pilate, **63** Saying, Sir, we remember that that deceiver said, while he was yet alive, After three days I will rise again.

Matthew 28

The Risen Christ

9 And as they went to tell his disciples, behold, Jesus met them, saying, All hail. And they came and held him by the feet, and worshipped him. **10** Then said Jesus unto them, Be not afraid: go tell my brethren that they go into Galilee, and there shall they see me.

Great Commission

18 And Jesus came and spake unto them, saying, All power is given unto me in heaven and in earth. **19** Go ye therefore, and teach all nations, baptizing them in the name of the Father, and of the Son, and of the Holy Ghost: **20** Teaching them to observe all things whatsoever I have commanded you: and, lo, I am with you alway, *even* unto the end of the world. Amen.

Mark

Mark 1

Preaching in Galilee and the Call of the Disciples

15 And saying, The time is fulfilled, and the kingdom of God is at hand: repent ye, and believe the gospel. **16** Now as he walked by the sea of Galilee, he saw Simon and Andrew his brother casting a net into the sea: for they were fishers. **17** And Jesus said unto them, Come ye after me, and I will make you to become fishers of men.

Jesus' Authority

25 And Jesus rebuked him, saying, Hold thy peace, and come out of him. **26** And when the unclean spirit had torn him, and cried with a loud voice, he came out of him.

Praying and Preaching

38 And he said unto them, Let us go into the next towns, that I may preach there also: for therefore came I forth.

Cleansing a Leper

40 And there came a leper to him, beseeching him, and kneeling down to him, and saying unto him, If thou wilt, thou canst make me clean. **41** And Jesus, moved with compassion, put forth his hand, and touched him, and saith unto him, I will; be thou clean. **42** And as soon as he had spoken, immediately the leprosy departed from him, and he was cleansed. **43** And he straitly charged him, and forthwith sent him away; **44** And saith unto him, See thou say nothing to any man: but go thy way, shew thyself to the priest, and offer for thy cleansing those things which

Moses commanded, for a testimony unto them.

Mark 2

Healing and Forgiving a Paralytic

5 When Jesus saw their faith, he said unto the sick of the palsy, Son, thy sins be forgiven thee. **6** But there were certain of the scribes sitting there, and reasoning in their hearts, **7** Why doth this man thus speak blasphemies? who can forgive sins but God only? **8** And immediately when Jesus perceived in his spirit that they so reasoned within themselves, he said unto them, Why reason ye these things in your hearts? **9** Whether is it easier to say to the sick of the palsy, Thy sins be forgiven thee; or to say, Arise, and take up thy bed, and walk? **10** But that ye may know that the Son of man hath power on earth to forgive sins, (he saith to the sick of the palsy,) **11** I say unto thee, Arise, and take up thy bed, and go thy way into thine house.

The Call of Levi; Eating with Sinners

14 And as he passed by, he saw Levi the son of Alphaeus sitting at the receipt of custom, and said unto him, Follow me. And he arose and followed him.

16 And when the scribes and Pharisees saw him eat with publicans and sinners, they said unto his disciples, How is it that he eateth and drinketh with publicans and sinners? **17** When Jesus heard it, he saith unto them, They that are whole have no need of the physician, but they that are sick: I came not to call the righteous, but sinners to repentance.

The Superiority of the New

18 And the disciples of John and of the Pharisees used to fast: and they come and say unto him, Why do the disciples of John and of the Pharisees fast, but thy disciples fast not? **19** And Jesus said unto them, Can the children of the bridechamber fast, while the bridegroom is with them? as long as they have the bridegroom with them, they cannot fast. **20** But the days will come, when the bridegroom shall be taken away from them, and then shall they fast in those days. **21** No man also seweth a piece of new cloth on an old garment: else the new piece that filled it up taketh away from the old, and the rent is made worse. **22** And no man putteth new wine into old bottles: else the new wine doth burst the bottles, and the wine is spilled, and the bottles will be marred: but new wine must be put into new bottles.

Lord of the Sabbath

25 And he said unto them, Have ye never read what David did, when he had need, and was an hungred, he, and they that were with him? **26** How he went into the house of God in the days of Abiathar the high priest, and did eat the shewbread, which is not lawful to eat but for the priests, and gave also to them which were with him? **27** And he said unto them, The sabbath was made for man, and not man for the sabbath: **28** Therefore the Son of man is Lord also of the sabbath.

Mark 3

Jesus Heals a Withered Hand

3 And he saith unto the man which had the withered hand, Stand forth. **4** And he saith unto them, Is it lawful to do good on the sabbath days, or to do evil? to save life, or to kill? But they held their peace. **5** And when he had looked round about on them with anger, being grieved for the hardness of their hearts, he saith unto the man, Stretch forth thine hand. And he stretched it out: and his hand was restored whole as the other.

A Divided Kingdom

23 And he called them unto him, and said unto them in parables, How can Satan cast out Satan? **24** And if a kingdom be divided against itself, that kingdom cannot stand. **25** And if a house be divided against itself, that house cannot stand. **26** And if Satan rise up against himself, and be divided, he cannot stand, but hath an end. **27** No man can enter into a strong man's house, and spoil his goods, except he will first bind the strong man; and then he will spoil his house. **28** Verily I say unto you, All sins shall be forgiven unto the sons of men, and blasphemies wherewith soever they shall blaspheme: **29** But he that shall blaspheme against the Holy Ghost hath never forgiveness, but is in danger of eternal damnation:

Jesus' Family

33 And he answered them, saying, Who is my mother, or my brethren? **34** And he looked round about on them which sat about him, and said, Behold my mother and my brethren! **35** For whosoever shall do the will of God, the same is my brother, and my sister, and mother.

Mark 4

The Parable of the Sower

2 And he taught them many things by parables, and said unto them in his doctrine, **3** Hearken; Behold, there went out a sower to sow: **4** And it came to pass, as he sowed, some fell by the way side, and the fowls of the air came and devoured it up. **5** And some fell on stony ground, where it had not much earth; and immediately it sprang up, because it had no depth of earth: **6** But when the sun was up, it was scorched; and because it had no root, it withered away. **7** And some fell among thorns, and the thorns grew up, and choked it, and it yielded no fruit. **8** And other fell on good ground, and did yield fruit that sprang up and increased; and brought forth, some thirty, and some sixty, and some an hundred. **9** And he said unto them, He that hath ears to hear, let him hear. **10** And when he was alone, they that were about him with the twelve asked of him the parable. **11** And he said unto them, Unto you it is given to know the mystery of the kingdom of God: but unto them that are without, all *these* things are done in parables: **12** **That seeing they may see, and not perceive; and hearing they may hear, and not**

understand; lest at any time they should be converted, and *their* sins should be forgiven them. **13** And he said unto them, Know ye not this parable? and how then will ye know all parables? **14** The sower soweth the word. **15** And these are they by the way side, where the word is sown; but when they have heard, Satan cometh immediately, and taketh away the word that was sown in their hearts. **16** And these are they likewise which are sown on stony ground; who, when they have heard the word, immediately receive it with gladness; **17** And have no root in themselves, and so endure but for a time: afterward, when affliction or persecution ariseth for the word's sake, immediately they are offended. **18** And these are they which are sown among thorns; such as hear the word, **19** And the cares of this world, and the deceitfulness of riches, and the lusts of other things entering in, choke the word, and it becometh unfruitful. **20** And these are they which are sown on good ground; such as hear the word, and receive *it*, and bring forth fruit, some thirtyfold, some sixty, and some an hundred.

The Parable of the Candle
21 And he said unto them, Is a candle brought to be put under a bushel, or under a bed? and not to be set on a candlestick? **22** For there is nothing hid, which shall not be manifested; neither was any thing kept secret, but that it should come abroad. **23** If any man have ears to hear, let him hear. **24** And he said unto them, Take heed what ye hear: with what measure ye mete, it shall be measured to you: and unto you that hear shall more be given. **25** For he that hath, to him shall be given: and he that hath not, from him shall be taken even that which he hath.

The Parable of the Growing Seed
26 And he said, So is the kingdom of God, as if a man should cast seed into the ground; **27** And should sleep, and rise night and day, and the seed should spring and grow up, he knoweth not how. **28** For the earth bringeth forth fruit of herself; first the blade, then the ear, after

that the full corn in the ear. **29** But when the fruit is brought forth, immediately he putteth in the sickle, because the harvest is come.

The Parable of the Mustard Seed

30 And he said, Whereunto shall we liken the kingdom of God? or with what comparison shall we compare it? **31** *It is* like a grain of mustard seed, which, when it is sown in the earth, is less than all the seeds that be in the earth: **32** But when it is sown, it groweth up, and becometh greater than all herbs, and shooteth out great branches; so that the fowls of the air may lodge under the shadow of it.

Jesus Rebukes the Wind

35 And the same day, when the even was come, he saith unto them, Let us pass over unto the other side.

39 And he arose, and rebuked the wind, and said unto the sea, Peace, be still. And the wind ceased, and there was a great calm. **40** And he said unto them, Why are ye so fearful? how is it that ye have no faith?

Mark 5

Healing of a Demoniac

8 For he said unto him, Come out of the man, thou unclean spirit. **9** And he asked him, What is thy name? And he answered, saying, My name *is* Legion: for we are many.

19 Howbeit Jesus suffered him not, but saith unto him, Go home to thy friends, and tell them how great things the Lord hath done for thee, and hath had compassion on thee.

Restoration and Healing of the Woman with Issue of Blood

30 And Jesus, immediately knowing in himself that virtue had gone out of him, turned him about in the press, and said, Who touched my clothes? **31** And his disciples said unto him, Thou seest the multitude thronging thee, and sayest thou, Who touched me? **32** And he looked round about to see her that had done this thing. 33 But the woman fearing and trembling, knowing what was done in her, came and fell down before him, and told him all the truth. 34 And he said unto her, Daughter, thy faith hath made thee whole; go in peace, and be whole of thy plague.

Jairus' Daughter Raised to Life

35 While he yet spake, there came from the ruler of the synagogue's house certain which said, Thy daughter is dead: why troublest thou the Master any further? 36 As soon as Jesus heard the word that was spoken, he saith unto the ruler of the synagogue, Be not afraid, only believe.

39 And when he was come in, he saith unto them, Why make ye this ado, and weep? the damsel is not dead, but sleepeth.

41 And he took the damsel by the hand, and said unto her, Talitha cumi; which is, being interpreted, Damsel, I say unto thee, arise. 42 And straightway the damsel arose, and walked; for she was of the age of twelve years. And they were astonished with a great astonishment.

Mark 6

Jesus' Rejection at Nazareth

3 Is not this the carpenter, the son of Mary, the brother of James, and Joses, and of Juda, and Simon? and are not his sisters here with us? And they were offended at him. 4 But Jesus said unto them, A prophet is not without honour, but in his own country, and among his own kin, and in his own house.

Sending Out the Disciples

10 And he said unto them, In what place soever ye enter into an house, there abide till ye depart from that place. 11 And whosoever shall not receive you, nor hear you, when ye depart thence, shake off the dust under your feet for a testimony against them. Verily I say unto you, It shall be more tolerable for Sodom and Gomorrha in the

day of judgment, than for that city.

The Feeding of the Five Thousand

31 And he said unto them, Come ye yourselves apart into a desert place, and rest a while: for there were many coming and going, and they had no leisure so much as to eat.

35 And when the day was now far spent, his disciples came unto him, and said, This is a desert place, and now the time is far passed: 36 Send them away, that they may go into the country round about, and into the villages, and buy themselves bread: for they have nothing to eat. 37 He answered and said unto them, Give ye them to eat. And they say unto him, Shall we go and buy two hundred pennyworth of bread, and give them to eat? 38 He saith unto them, How many loaves have ye? go and see. And when they knew, they say, Five, and two fishes.

Jesus Walks on the Sea

49 But when they saw him walking upon the sea, they supposed it had been a spirit, and cried out: 50 For they all saw him, and were troubled. And immediately he talked with them, and saith unto them, Be of good cheer: it is I; be not afraid.

Mark 7

Breaking Human Traditions

5 Then the Pharisees and scribes asked him, Why walk not thy disciples according to the tradition of the elders, but eat bread with unwashen hands? 6 He answered and said unto them, Well hath Esaias prophesied of you hypocrites, as it is written, **This people honoureth me with *their* lips, but their heart is far from me. 7 Howbeit in vain do they worship me, teaching *for* doctrines the commandments of men.** 8 For laying aside the commandment of God, ye hold the tradition of men, *as* the washing of pots and cups: and many other such like things ye do. 9 And he said unto them, Full well

ye reject the commandment of God, that ye may keep your own tradition. **10** For Moses said, **Honour thy father and thy mother;** and, **Whoso curseth father or mother, let him die the death: 11** But ye say, If a man shall say to his father or mother, *It is* Corban, that is to say, a gift, by whatsoever thou mightest be profited by me; *he shall be free.* **12** And ye suffer him no more to do ought for his father or his mother; **13** Making the word of God of none effect through your tradition, which ye have delivered: and many such like things do ye.

Things from Within Defile

14 And when he had called all the people unto him, he said unto them, Hearken unto me every one *of you*, and understand: **15** There is nothing from without a man, that entering into him can defile him: but the things which come out of him, those are they that defile the man. **16** If any man have ears to hear, let him hear. **17** And when he was entered into the house from the people, his disciples asked him concerning the parable. **18** And he saith unto them, Are ye so without understanding also? Do ye not perceive, that whatsoever thing from without entereth into the man, *it* cannot defile him; **19** Because it entereth not into his heart, but into the belly, and goeth out into the draught, purging all meats? **20** And he said, That which cometh out of the man, that defileth the man. **21** For from within, out of the heart of men, proceed evil thoughts, adulteries, fornications, murders, **22** Thefts, covetousness, wickedness, deceit, lasciviousness, an evil eye, blasphemy, pride, foolishness: **23** All these evil things come from within, and defile the man.

A Syrophoenician Woman's Faith

26 The woman was a Greek, a Syrophenician by nation; and she besought him that he would cast forth the devil out of her daughter. **27** But Jesus said unto her, Let the children first be filled: for it is not meet to take the children's bread, and to cast *it* unto the dogs. **28** And she answered and said unto him, Yes, Lord: yet the dogs under the table eat of the children's crumbs. **29** And he said unto her, For this saying go thy way; the devil is gone out of thy daughter.

Healing a Deaf Mute
34 And looking up to heaven, he sighed, and saith unto him, Ephphatha, that is, Be opened. **35** And straightway his ears were opened, and the string of his tongue was loosed, and he spake plain.

Mark 8

The Feeding of the Four Thousand
2 I have compassion on the multitude, because they have now been with me three days, and have nothing to eat: **3** And if I send them away fasting to their own houses, they will faint by the way: for divers of them came from far. **4** And his disciples answered him, From whence can a man satisfy these *men* with bread here in the wilderness? **5** And he asked them, How many loaves have ye? And they said, Seven.

The Demand for a Sign
12 And he sighed deeply in his spirit, and saith, Why doth this generation seek after a sign? verily I say unto you, There shall no sign be given unto this generation.

The Leaven of the Pharisees
14 Now the disciples had forgotten to take bread, neither had they in the ship with them more than one loaf. **15** And he charged them, saying, Take heed, beware of the leaven of the Pharisees, and of the leaven of Herod. **16** And they reasoned among themselves, saying, It is because we have no bread. **17** And when Jesus knew it, he saith unto them, Why reason ye, because ye have no bread? perceive ye not yet, neither understand? have ye your heart yet hardened? **18** Having eyes, see ye not? and having ears,

hear ye not? and do ye not remember? **19** When I brake the five loaves among five thousand, how many baskets full of fragments took ye up? They say unto him, Twelve. **20** And when the seven among four thousand, how many baskets full of fragments took ye up? And they said, Seven. **21** And he said unto them, How is it that ye do not understand?

Jesus Heals a Blind Man at Bethsaida
25 After that he put his hands again upon his eyes, and made him look up: and he was restored, and saw every man clearly. **26** And he sent him away to his house, saying, Neither go into the town, nor tell *it* to any in the town.

Peter's Confession and Prediction of Jesus' Death
27 And Jesus went out, and his disciples, into the towns of Caesarea Philippi: and by the way he asked his disciples, saying unto them, Whom do men say that I am? **28** And they answered, John the Baptist: but some *say*, Elias; and others, One of the prophets. **29** And he saith unto them, But whom say ye that I am? And Peter answereth and saith unto him, Thou art the Christ.

33 But when he had turned about and looked on his disciples, he rebuked Peter, saying, Get thee behind me, Satan: for thou savourest not the things that be of God, but the things that be of men.

Following Jesus
34 And when he had called the people unto him with his disciples also, he said unto them, Whosoever will come after me, let him deny himself, and take up his cross, and follow me. **35** For whosoever will save his life shall lose it; but whosoever shall lose his life for my sake and the gospel's, the same shall save it. **36** For what shall it profit a man, if he shall gain the whole world, and lose his own soul? **37** Or what shall a man give in exchange for his soul? **38** Whosoever therefore shall be ashamed of me and of my words in this adulterous and sinful generation; of him

also shall the Son of man be ashamed, when he cometh in the glory of his Father with the holy angels.

Mark 9

1 And he said unto them, Verily I say unto you, That there be some of them that stand here, which shall not taste of death, till they have seen the kingdom of God come with power.

Jesus' Transfiguration
12 And he answered and told them, Elias verily cometh first, and restoreth all things; and how it is written of the Son of man, that he must suffer many things, and be set at nought. **13** But I say unto you, That Elias is indeed come, and they have done unto him whatsoever they listed, as it is written of him.

A Dumb and Deaf Spirit Cast Out
16 And he asked the scribes, What question ye with them? **17** And one of the multitude answered and said, Master, I have brought unto thee my son, which hath a dumb spirit; **18** And wheresoever he taketh him, he teareth him: and he foameth, and gnasheth with his teeth, and pineth away: and I spake to thy disciples that they should cast him out; and they could not. **19** He answereth him, and saith, O faithless generation, how long shall I be with you? how long shall I suffer you? bring him unto me. **20** And they brought him unto him: and when he saw him, straightway the spirit tare him; and he fell on the ground, and wallowed foaming. **21** And he asked his father, How long is it ago since this came unto him? And he said, Of a child. **22** And ofttimes it hath cast him into the fire, and into the waters, to destroy him: but if thou canst do any thing, have compassion on us, and help us. **23** Jesus said unto him, If thou canst believe, all things are possible to him that believeth. **24** And straightway the father of the child cried out, and said with tears, Lord, I believe; help thou mine unbelief. **25** When Jesus saw that the people

came running together, he rebuked the foul spirit, saying unto him, Thou dumb and deaf spirit, I charge thee, come out of him, and enter no more into him. 26 And the spirit cried, and rent him sore, and came out of him: and he was as one dead; insomuch that many said, He is dead. 27 But Jesus took him by the hand, and lifted him up; and he arose. 28 And when he was come into the house, his disciples asked him privately, Why could not we cast him out? 29 And he said unto them, This kind can come forth by nothing, but by prayer and fasting.

Prediction of Jesus' Death

31 For he taught his disciples, and said unto them, The Son of man is delivered into the hands of men, and they shall kill him; and after that he is killed, he shall rise the third day.

Questions About the Greatest

33 And he came to Capernaum: and being in the house he asked them, What was it that ye disputed among yourselves by the way?

35 And he sat down, and called the twelve, and saith unto them, If any man desire to be first, the same shall be last of all, and servant of all. 36 And he took a child, and set him in the midst of them: and when he had taken him in his arms, he said unto them, 37 Whosoever shall receive one of such children in my name, receiveth me: and whosoever shall receive me, receiveth not me, but him that sent me.

On Jesus' Side

38 And John answered him, saying, Master, we saw one casting out devils in thy name, and he followeth not us: and we forbad him, because he followeth not us. 39 But Jesus said, Forbid him not: for there is no man which shall do a miracle in my name, that can lightly speak evil of me. 40 For he that is not against us is on our part. 41 For whosoever shall give you a cup of water to drink in my name, because ye belong to Christ, verily I say unto you,

he shall not lose his reward.

Jesus Warns against Temptation

42 And whosoever shall offend one of these little ones that believe in me, it is better for him that a millstone were hanged about his neck, and he were cast into the sea. **43** And if thy hand offend thee, cut it off: it is better for thee to enter into life maimed, than having two hands to go into hell, into the fire that never shall be quenched: **44 Where their worm dieth not, and the fire is not quenched.** **45** And if thy foot offend thee, cut it off: it is better for thee to enter halt into life, than having two feet to be cast into hell, into the fire that never shall be quenched: **46** Where their worm dieth not, and the fire is not quenched. **47** And if thine eye offend thee, pluck it out: it is better for thee to enter into the kingdom of God with one eye, than having two eyes to be cast into hell fire: **48** Where their worm dieth not, and the fire is not quenched. **49** For every one shall be salted with fire, and every sacrifice shall be salted with salt. **50** Salt *is* good: but if the salt have lost his saltness, wherewith will ye season it? Have salt in yourselves, and have peace one with another.

Mark
10

Marriage and Divorce

2 And the Pharisees came to him, and asked him, Is it lawful for a man to put away his wife? tempting him. **3** And he answered and said unto them, What did Moses command you? **4** And they said, Moses suffered to write a bill of divorcement, and to put her away. **5** And Jesus answered and said unto them, For the hardness of your heart he wrote you this precept. **6** But from the beginning of the creation **God made them male and female. 7 For this cause shall a man leave his father and mother, and cleave to his wife; 8 And they twain shall be one flesh: so then they are no more twain, but one flesh. 9** What therefore God hath joined together, let not man put asunder. **10** And in the house his disciples asked him again of the same matter. **11** And he saith unto them, Whosoever shall put away his wife, and marry another, committeth adultery against her. **12** And if a woman shall put away her husband, and be married to another, she committeth adultery.

Jesus and Little Children

14 But when Jesus saw it, he was much displeased, and said unto them, Suffer the little children to come unto me, and forbid them not: for of such is the kingdom of God. **15** Verily I say unto you, Whosoever shall not receive the kingdom of God as a little child, he shall not enter therein.

The Rich Young Man

17 And when he was gone forth into the way, there came one running, and kneeled to him, and asked him, Good Master, what shall I do that I may inherit eternal life? **18** And Jesus said unto him, Why callest thou me good? there is none good but one, that is, God. **19** Thou knowest the commandments, Do not commit adultery, Do not kill, Do not steal, Do not bear false witness, Defraud not, Honour thy father and mother. **20** And he answered and said unto him, Master, all these have I observed from my youth. **21** Then Jesus beholding him loved him, and said unto him, One thing thou lackest: go thy way, sell whatsoever thou hast, and give to the poor, and thou shalt have treasure in heaven: and come, take up the cross, and follow me. **22** And he was sad at that saying, and went away grieved: for he had great possessions. **23** And Jesus looked round about, and saith unto his disciples, How hardly shall they that have riches enter into the kingdom of God! **24** And the disciples were astonished at his words. But Jesus answereth again, and saith unto them, Children, how hard is it for them that trust in riches to enter into the kingdom of God! **25** It is easier for a camel to go through the eye of a needle, than for a rich man to enter into the kingdom of God. **26** And they were astonished out of measure, saying among themselves, Who then can be saved? **27** And Jesus looking upon them saith, With men it is impossible, but not with God: for with God all things are possible. **28** Then Peter began to say unto him, Lo, we have left all, and have followed thee. **29** And Jesus answered and said, Verily I say unto you, There is no man that hath left house, or brethren, or sisters, or father, or mother, or wife, or children, or lands, for my sake, and the gospel's, **30** But he shall receive an hundredfold now in this time, houses, and brethren, and sisters, and mothers, and children, and lands, with persecutions; and in the world to come eternal life. **31** But many that are first shall be last; and the last first.

Prediction of Jesus' Death and Resurrection
33 Saying, Behold, we go up to Jerusalem; and the Son of man shall be delivered unto the chief priests, and unto the scribes; and they shall condemn him to death, and shall deliver him to the Gentiles: **34** And they shall mock him, and shall scourge him, and shall spit upon him, and shall kill him: and the third day he shall rise again.

James and John's Request
36 And he said unto them, What would ye that I should do for you? **37** They said unto him, Grant unto us that we may sit, one on thy right hand, and the other on thy left hand, in thy glory. **38** But Jesus said unto them, Ye know not what ye ask: can ye drink of the cup that I drink of? and be baptized with the baptism that I am baptized with? **39** And they said unto him, We can. And Jesus said unto them, Ye shall indeed drink of the cup that I drink of; and with the baptism that I am baptized withal shall ye be baptized: **40** But to sit on my right hand and on my left hand is not mine to give; but it shall be given to them for whom it is prepared. **41** And when the ten heard *it*, they began to be much displeased with James and John. **42** But Jesus called them to him, and saith unto them, Ye know that they which are accounted to rule over the Gentiles exercise lordship over them; and their great ones exercise authority upon them. **43** But so shall it not be

among you: but whosoever will be great among you, shall be your minister: **44** And whosoever of you will be the chiefest, shall be servant of all. **45** For even the Son of man came not to be ministered unto, but to minister, and to give his life a ransom for many.

Healing Blind Bartimaeus

51 And Jesus answered and said unto him, What wilt thou that I should do unto thee? The blind man said unto him, Lord, that I might receive my sight. **52** And Jesus said unto him, Go thy way; thy faith hath made thee whole. And immediately he received his sight, and followed Jesus in the way.

Mark 11

The Triumphal Entry

1 And when they came nigh to Jerusalem, unto Bethphage and Bethany, at the mount of Olives, he sendeth forth two of his disciples, **2** And saith unto them, Go your way into the village over against you: and as soon as ye be entered into it, ye shall find a colt tied, whereon never man sat; loose him, and bring him. **3** And if any man say unto you, Why do ye this? say ye that the Lord hath need of him; and straightway he will send him hither.

A Fig Tree Rebuked

12 And on the morrow, when they were come from Bethany, he was hungry: **13** And seeing a fig tree afar off having leaves, he came, if haply he might find any thing thereon: and when he came to it, he found nothing but leaves; for the time of figs was not yet. **14** And Jesus answered and said unto it, No man eat fruit of thee hereafter for ever. And his disciples heard it.

Cleansing the Temple

17 And he taught, saying unto them, Is it not written, **My house shall be called of all nations the house of**

prayer? but ye have made it a den of thieves.

The Lesson of the Fig Tree

20 And in the morning, as they passed by, they saw the fig tree dried up from the roots. **21** And Peter calling to remembrance saith unto him, Master, behold, the fig tree which thou cursedst is withered away. **22** And Jesus answering saith unto them, Have faith in God. **23** For verily I say unto you, That whosoever shall say unto this mountain, Be thou removed, and be thou cast into the sea; and shall not doubt in his heart, but shall believe that those things which he saith shall come to pass; he shall have whatsoever he saith. **24** Therefore I say unto you, What things soever ye desire, when ye pray, believe that ye receive them, and ye shall have them. **25** And when ye stand praying, forgive, if ye have ought against any: that your Father also which is in heaven may forgive you your trespasses. **26** But if ye do not forgive, neither will your Father which is in heaven forgive your trespasses.

Jesus' Authority Questioned

28 And say unto him, By what authority doest thou these things? and who gave thee this authority to do these things? **29** And Jesus answered and said unto them, I will also ask of you one question, and answer me, and I will tell you by what authority I do these things. **30** The baptism of John, was *it* from heaven, or of men? answer me. **31** And they reasoned with themselves, saying, If we shall say, From heaven; he will say, Why then did ye not believe him? **32** But if we shall say, Of men; they feared the people: for all *men* counted John, that he was a prophet indeed. **33** And they answered and said unto Jesus, We cannot tell. And Jesus answering saith unto them, Neither do I tell you by what authority I do these things.

Mark 12

The Parable of the Vineyard

1 And he began to speak unto them by parables. A certain man planted a vineyard, and set an hedge about it, and digged a place for the winefat, and built a tower, and let it out to husbandmen, and went into a far country. **2** And at the season he sent to the husbandmen a servant, that he might receive from the husbandmen of the fruit of the vineyard. **3** And they caught him, and beat him, and sent him away empty. **4** And again he sent unto them another servant; and at him they cast stones, and wounded him in the head, and sent him away shamefully handled. **5** And again he sent another; and him they killed, and many others; beating some, and killing some. **6** Having yet therefore one son, his wellbeloved, he sent him also last unto them, saying, They will reverence my son. **7** But those husbandmen said among themselves, This is the heir; come, let us kill him, and the inheritance shall be ours. **8** And they took him, and killed him, and cast him out of the vineyard. **9** What shall therefore the lord of the vineyard do? he will come and destroy the husbandmen, and will give the vineyard unto others. **10** And have ye not read this scripture; **The stone which the builders rejected is become the head of the corner: 11 This was the Lord's doing, and it is marvellous in our eyes?**

Paying Tribute to Caesar

15 Shall we give, or shall we not give? But he, knowing their hypocrisy, said unto them, Why tempt ye me? bring me a penny, that I may see it. **16** And they brought *it*. And he saith unto them, Whose is this image and superscription? And they said unto him, Caesar's. **17** And Jesus answering said unto them, Render to Caesar the things that are Caesar's, and to God the things that are God's. And they marvelled at him.

Marriage and the Resurrection

24 And Jesus answering said unto them, Do ye not therefore err, because ye know not the scriptures, neither the power of God? **25** For when they shall rise from the dead, they neither marry, nor are given in marriage; but are as the angels which are in heaven. 26 And as touching the dead, that they rise: have ye not read in the book of Moses, how in the bush God spake unto him, saying, **I am the God of Abraham, and the God of Isaac, and the God of Jacob?** 27 He is not the God of the dead, but the God of the living: ye therefore do greatly err.

The Greatest Commandment

28 And one of the scribes came, and having heard them reasoning together, and perceiving that he had answered them well, asked him, Which is the first commandment of all? **29** And Jesus answered him, The first of all the commandments is, **Hear, O Israel; The Lord our God is one Lord: 30 And thou shalt love the Lord thy God with all thy heart, and with all thy soul, and with all thy mind, and with all thy strength:** this is the first commandment. **31** And the second is like, namely this, **Thou shalt love thy neighbour as thyself.** There is none other commandment greater than these. **32** And the scribe said unto him, Well, Master, thou hast said the truth: for there is one God; and there is none other but he: **33** And to love him with all the heart, and with all the understanding, and with all the soul, and with all the strength, and to love his neighbour as himself, is more than all whole burnt offerings and sacrifices. **34** And when Jesus saw that he answered discreetly, he said unto him, Thou art not far from the kingdom of God. And no man after that durst ask him any question.

The Messiah: David's Son and Lord

35 And Jesus answered and said, while he taught in the temple, How say the scribes that Christ is the Son of David? **36** For David himself said by the Holy Ghost, **The LORD said to my Lord, Sit thou on my right hand, till I make thine enemies thy footstool.** **37** David therefore himself calleth him Lord; and whence is he then his son? And the common people heard him gladly. **38** And he said unto them in his doctrine, Beware of the scribes, which

love to go in long clothing, and love salutations in the marketplaces, **39** And the chief seats in the synagogues, and the uppermost rooms at feasts: **40** Which devour widows' houses, and for a pretence make long prayers: these shall receive greater damnation.

The Widow's Offering

43 And he called unto him his disciples, and saith unto them, Verily I say unto you, That this poor widow hath cast more in, than all they which have cast into the treasury: **44** For all they did cast in of their abundance; but she of her want did cast in all that she had, even all her living.

Mark 13

Signs of the End Times

2 And Jesus answering said unto him, Seest thou these great buildings? there shall not be left one stone upon another, that shall not be thrown down.

5 And Jesus answering them began to say, Take heed lest any man deceive you: **6** For many shall come in my name, saying, I am Christ; and shall deceive many. **7** And when ye shall hear of wars and rumours of wars, be ye not troubled: for such things must needs be; but the end shall not be yet. **8** For nation shall rise against nation, and kingdom against kingdom: and there shall be earthquakes in divers places, and there shall be famines and troubles: these are the beginnings of sorrows. **9** But take heed to yourselves: for they shall deliver you up to councils; and in the synagogues ye shall be beaten: and ye shall be brought before rulers and kings for my sake, for a testimony against them. **10** And the gospel must first be published among all nations. **11** But when they shall lead you, and deliver you up, take no thought beforehand what ye shall speak, neither do ye premeditate: but whatsoever shall be given you in that hour, that speak ye: for it is not ye that speak, but the Holy Ghost. **12** Now the brother shall betray the brother to death, and the father the son; and children shall rise up against their parents, and shall cause them to be put to death. 13 And ye shall be hated of all men for my name's sake: but he that shall endure unto the end, the same shall be saved.

14 But when ye shall see the abomination of desolation, spoken of by Daniel the prophet, standing where it ought not, (let him that readeth understand,) then let them that be in Judaea flee to the mountains: 15 And let him that is on the housetop not go down into the house, neither enter therein, to take any thing out of his house: 16 And let him that is in the field not turn back again for to take up his garment. 17 But woe to them that are with child, and to them that give suck in those days! 18 And pray ye that your flight be not in the winter. 19 For in those days shall be affliction, such as was not from the beginning of the creation which God created unto this time, neither shall be. 20 And except that the Lord had shortened those days, no flesh should be saved: but for the elect's sake, whom he hath chosen, he hath shortened the days. 21 And then if any man shall say to you, Lo, here is Christ; or, lo, he is there; believe him not: 22 For false Christs and false prophets shall rise, and shall shew signs and wonders, to seduce, if it were possible, even the elect. 23 But take ye heed: behold, I have foretold you all things.

The Arrival of the Son of Man

24 But in those days, after that tribulation, the sun shall be darkened, and the moon shall not give her light, 25 And the stars of heaven shall fall, and the powers that are in heaven shall be shaken. 26 And then shall they see the Son of man coming in the clouds with great power and glory. 27 And then shall he send his angels, and shall gather together his elect from the four winds, from the uttermost part of the earth to the uttermost part of heaven.

28 Now learn a parable of the fig tree; When her branch is yet tender, and putteth forth leaves, ye know that summer is near: 29 So ye in like manner, when ye shall

see these things come to pass, know that it is nigh, at the doors. **30** Verily I say unto you, that this generation shall not pass, till all these things be done. **31** Heaven and earth shall pass away: but my words shall not pass away.

Watch and Pray

32 But of that day and that hour knoweth no man, no, not the angels which are in heaven, neither the Son, but the Father. **33** Take ye heed, watch and pray: for ye know not when the time is. **34** For the Son of man is as a man taking a far journey, who left his house, and gave authority to his servants, and to every man his work, and commanded the porter to watch. **35** Watch ye therefore: for ye know not when the master of the house cometh, at even, or at midnight, or at the cockcrowing, or in the morning: **36** Lest coming suddenly he find you sleeping. **37** And what I say unto you I say unto all, Watch.

Mark 14

A Woman Anoints Jesus

6 And Jesus said, Let her alone; why trouble ye her? she hath wrought a good work on me. **7** For ye have the poor with you always, and whensoever ye will ye may do them good: but me ye have not always. **8** She hath done what she could: she is come aforehand to anoint my body to the burying. **9** Verily I say unto you, Wheresoever this gospel shall be preached throughout the whole world, this also that she hath done shall be spoken of for a memorial of her.

The Passover Prepared

12 And the first day of unleavened bread, when they killed the passover, his disciples said unto him, Where wilt thou that we go and prepare that thou mayest eat the passover? **13** And he sendeth forth two of his disciples, and saith unto them, Go ye into the city, and there shall meet you a man bearing a pitcher of water: follow him. **14**

And wheresoever he shall go in, say ye to the goodman of the house, The Master saith, Where is the guestchamber, where I shall eat the passover with my disciples? **15** And he will shew you a large upper room furnished and prepared: there make ready for us. **16** And his disciples went forth, and came into the city, and found as he had said unto them: and they made ready the passover. **17** And in the evening he cometh with the twelve. **18** And as they sat and did eat, Jesus said, Verily I say unto you, One of you which eateth with me shall betray me. **19** And they began to be sorrowful, and to say unto him one by one, Is it I? and another said, Is it I? **20** And he answered and said unto them, It is one of the twelve, that dippeth with me in the dish. **21** The Son of man indeed goeth, as it is written of him: but woe to that man by whom the Son of man is betrayed! good were it for that man if he had never been born.

The Lord's Supper
22 And as they did eat, Jesus took bread, and blessed, and brake it, and gave to them, and said, Take, eat: this is my body. **23** And he took the cup, and when he had given thanks, he gave it to them: and they all drank of it. **24** And he said unto them, This is my blood of the new testament, which is shed for many. **25** Verily I say unto you, I will drink no more of the fruit of the vine, until that day that I drink it new in the kingdom of God. **26** And when they had sung an hymn, they went out into the mount of Olives.

The Prediction of Peter's Denial
27 And Jesus saith unto them, All ye shall be offended because of me this night: for it is written, **I will smite the shepherd, and the sheep shall be scattered. 28** But after that I am risen, I will go before you into Galilee. **29** But Peter said unto him, Although all shall be offended, yet will not I. **30** And Jesus saith unto him, Verily I say unto thee, That this day, even in this night, before the cock crow twice, thou shalt deny me thrice.

Gethsemane

32 And they came to a place which was named Gethsemane: and he saith to his disciples, Sit ye here, while I shall pray. **33** And he taketh with him Peter and James and John, and began to be sore amazed, and to be very heavy; **34** And saith unto them, My soul is exceeding sorrowful unto death: tarry ye here, and watch. **35** And he went forward a little, and fell on the ground, and prayed that, if it were possible, the hour might pass from him. **36** And he said, Abba, Father, all things are possible unto thee; take away this cup from me: nevertheless not what I will, but what thou wilt. **37** And he cometh, and findeth them sleeping, and saith unto Peter, Simon, sleepest thou? couldest not thou watch one hour? **38** Watch ye and pray, lest ye enter into temptation. The spirit truly is ready, but the flesh *is* weak. **39** And again he went away, and prayed, and spake the same words. **40** And when he returned, he found them asleep again, (for their eyes were heavy,) neither wist they what to answer him. **41** And he cometh the third time, and saith unto them, Sleep on now, and take your rest: it is enough, the hour is come; behold, the Son of man is betrayed into the hands of sinners. **42** Rise up, let us go; lo, he that betrayeth me is at hand.

Jesus' Arrest

48 And Jesus answered and said unto them, Are ye come out, as against a thief, with swords and with staves to take me? **49** I was daily with you in the temple teaching, and ye took me not: but the scriptures must be fulfilled.

Condemned by the Sanhedrin

61 But he held his peace, and answered nothing. Again the high priest asked him, and said unto him, Art thou the Christ, the Son of the Blessed? **62** And Jesus said, I am: and ye shall see the Son of man sitting on the right hand of power, and coming in the clouds of heaven.

Peter's Denials

72 And the second time the cock crew. And Peter called to mind the word that Jesus said unto him, Before the cock crow twice, thou shalt deny me thrice. And when he thought thereon, he wept.

Mark 15

Jesus' Trial Before Pilate

2 And Pilate asked him, Art thou the King of the Jews? And he answering said unto him, Thou sayest it.

Jesus is Crucified at Golgotha

34 And at the ninth hour Jesus cried with a loud voice, saying, **Eloi, Eloi, lama sabachthani?** which is, being interpreted, **My God, my God, why hast thou forsaken me?**

Mark 16

Jesus' Commission of the Eleven

15 And he said unto them, Go ye into all the world, and preach the gospel to every creature. **16** He that believeth and is baptized shall be saved; but he that believeth not shall be damned. **17** And these signs shall follow them that believe; In my name shall they cast out devils; they shall speak with new tongues; **18** They shall take up serpents; and if they drink any deadly thing, it shall not hurt them; they shall lay hands on the sick, and they shall recover.

Luke

Luke 2

Jesus' Converses with Teachers in the Temple

49 And he said unto them, How is it that ye sought me? wist ye not that I must be about my Father's business?

Luke 4

The Temptation of Jesus

3 And the devil said unto him, If thou be the Son of God, command this stone that it be made bread. 4 And Jesus answered him, saying, It is written, **That man shall not live by bread alone, but by every word of God.** 5 And the devil, taking him up into an high mountain, shewed unto him all the kingdoms of the world in a moment of time. 6 And the devil said unto him, All this power will I give thee, and the glory of them: for that is delivered unto me; and to whomsoever I will I give it. 7 If thou therefore wilt worship me, all shall be thine. 8 And Jesus answered and said unto him, Get thee behind me, Satan: for it is written, **Thou shalt worship the Lord thy God, and him only shalt thou serve.** 9 And he brought him to Jerusalem, and set him on a pinnacle of the temple, and said unto him, If thou be the Son of God, cast thyself down from hence: 10 For it is written, **He shall give his angels charge over thee, to keep thee:** 11 **And in** *their* **hands they shall bear thee up, lest at any time thou dash thy foot against a stone.** 12 And Jesus answering said unto

him, It is said, **Thou shalt not tempt the Lord thy God.**
13 And when the devil had ended all the temptation, he departed from him for a season.

The Beginning of Jesus' Ministry in Galilee

17 And there was delivered unto him the book of the prophet Esaias. And when he had opened the book, he found the place where it was written, **18 The Spirit of the Lord is upon me, because he hath anointed me to preach the gospel to the poor; he hath sent me to heal the brokenhearted, to preach deliverance to the captives, and recovering of sight to the blind, to set at liberty them that are bruised, 19 To preach the acceptable year of the Lord.** 20 And he closed the book, and he gave *it* again to the minister, and sat down. And the eyes of all them that were in the synagogue were fastened on him. 21 And he began to say unto them, This day is this scripture fulfilled in your ears. 22 And all bare him witness, and wondered at the gracious words which proceeded out of his mouth. And they said, Is not this Joseph's son? 23 And he said unto them, Ye will surely say unto me this proverb, Physician, heal thyself: whatsoever we have heard done in Capernaum, do also here in thy country. 24 And he said, Verily I say unto you, No prophet is accepted in his own country. 25 But I tell you of a truth, many widows were in Israel in the days of Elias, when the heaven was shut up three years and six months, when great famine was throughout all the land; 26 But unto none of them was Elias sent, save unto Sarepta, a city of Sidon, unto a woman that was a widow. 27 And many lepers were in Israel in the time of Eliseus the prophet; and none of them was cleansed, saving Naaman the Syrian.

Healing a Man with Unclean Devil

33 And in the synagogue there was a man, which had a spirit of an unclean devil, and cried out with a loud voice, 34 Saying, Let us alone; what have we to do with thee, thou Jesus of Nazareth? art thou come to destroy us? I

know thee who thou art; the Holy One of God. **35** And Jesus rebuked him, saying, Hold thy peace, and come out of him. And when the devil had thrown him in the midst, he came out of him, and hurt him not.

42 And when it was day, he departed and went into a desert place: and the people sought him, and came unto him, and stayed him, that he should not depart from them. **43** And he said unto them, I must preach the kingdom of God to other cities also: for therefore am I sent.

Luke 5

Fishermen Follow Jesus

3 And he entered into one of the ships, which was Simon's, and prayed him that he would thrust out a little from the land. And he sat down, and taught the people out of the ship. **4** Now when he had left speaking, he said unto Simon, Launch out into the deep, and let down your nets for a draught.

10 And so was also James, and John, the sons of Zebedee, which were partners with Simon. And Jesus said unto Simon, Fear not; from henceforth thou shalt catch men. **11** And when they had brought their ships to land, they forsook all, and followed him.

Healing a Leper

13 And he put forth his hand, and touched him, saying, I will: be thou clean. And immediately the leprosy departed from him. **14** And he charged him to tell no man: but go, and shew thyself to the priest, and offer for thy cleansing, according as Moses commanded, for a testimony unto them.

Healing and Forgiving a Paralytic

20 And when he saw their faith, he said unto him, Man, thy sins are forgiven thee. **21** And the scribes and the

Pharisees began to reason, saying, Who is this which speaketh blasphemies? Who can forgive sins, but God alone? **22** But when Jesus perceived their thoughts, he answering said unto them, What reason ye in your hearts? **23** Whether is easier, to say, Thy sins be forgiven thee; or to say, Rise up and walk? **24** But that ye may know that the Son of man hath power upon earth to forgive sins, (he said unto the sick of the palsy,) I say unto thee, Arise, and take up thy couch, and go into thine house. **25** And immediately he rose up before them, and took up that whereon he lay, and departed to his own house, glorifying God.

The Call of Levi; Eating with Sinners

27 And after these things he went forth, and saw a publican, named Levi, sitting at the receipt of custom: and he said unto him, Follow me. **28** And he left all, rose up, and followed him. **29** And Levi made him a great feast in his own house: and there was a great company of publicans and of others that sat down with them. **30** But their scribes and Pharisees murmured against his disciples, saying, Why do ye eat and drink with publicans and sinners? **31** And Jesus answering said unto them, They that are whole need not a physician; but they that are sick. **32** I came not to call the righteous, but sinners to repentance. **33** And they said unto him, Why do the disciples of John fast often, and make prayers, and likewise the disciples of the Pharisees; but thine eat and drink? **34** And he said unto them, Can ye make the children of the bridechamber fast, while the bridegroom is with them? **35** But the days will come, when the bridegroom shall be taken away from them, and then shall they fast in those days. **36** And he spake also a parable unto them; No man putteth a piece of a new garment upon an old; if otherwise, then both the new maketh a rent, and the piece that was taken out of the new agreeth not with the old. **37** And no man putteth new wine into old bottles; else the new wine will burst the bottles, and be spilled, and the bottles shall perish. **38** But new wine must be put into new bottles; and both are preserved. **39** No man also having drunk old wine straightway desireth new: for he saith, The old is better.

Luke
6

Lord of the Sabbath

3 And Jesus answering them said, Have ye not read so much as this, what David did, when himself was an hungred, and they which were with him; **4** How he went into the house of God, and did take and eat the shewbread, and gave also to them that were with him; which it is not lawful to eat but for the priests alone? **5** And he said unto them, That the Son of man is Lord also of the sabbath.

8 But he knew their thoughts, and said to the man which had the withered hand, Rise up, and stand forth in the midst. And he arose and stood forth. **9** Then said Jesus unto them, I will ask you one thing; Is it lawful on the sabbath days to do good, or to do evil? to save life, or to destroy it? **10** And looking round about upon them all, he said unto the man, Stretch forth thy hand. And he did so: and his hand was restored whole as the other.

Beatitude

20 And he lifted up his eyes on his disciples, and said, Blessed be ye poor: for yours is the kingdom of God. **21** Blessed are ye that hunger now: for ye shall be filled. Blessed are ye that weep now: for ye shall laugh. **22** Blessed are ye, when men shall hate you, and when they shall separate you from their company, and shall reproach you, and cast out your name as evil, for the Son of man's sake. **23** Rejoice ye in that day, and leap for joy: for, behold, your reward is great in heaven: for in the like manner did their fathers unto the prophets. **24** But woe unto you that are rich! for ye have received your consolation. **25** Woe unto you that are full! for ye shall hunger. Woe unto you that laugh now! for ye shall mourn and weep. **26** Woe unto you, when all men shall speak well of you! for so did their fathers to the false prophets.

27 But I say unto you which hear, Love your enemies, do good to them which hate you, **28** Bless them that curse you, and pray for them which despitefully use you. **29** And unto him that smiteth thee on the one cheek offer also the other; and him that taketh away thy cloke forbid not to take thy coat also. **30** Give to every man that asketh of thee; and of him that taketh away thy goods ask them not again. **31** And as ye would that men should do to you, do ye also to them likewise. **32** For if ye love them which love you, what thank have ye? for sinners also love those that love them. **33** And if ye do good to them which do good to you, what thank have ye? for sinners also do even the same. **34** And if ye lend to them of whom ye hope to receive, what thank have ye? for sinners also lend to sinners, to receive as much again. **35** But love ye your enemies, and do good, and lend, hoping for nothing again; and your reward shall be great, and ye shall be the children of the Highest: for he is kind unto the unthankful and to the evil. **36** Be ye therefore merciful, as your Father also is merciful.

37 Judge not, and ye shall not be judged: condemn not, and ye shall not be condemned: forgive, and ye shall be forgiven: **38** Give, and it shall be given unto you; good measure, pressed down, and shaken together, and running over, shall men give into your bosom. For with the same measure that ye mete withal it shall be measured to you again. **39** And he spake a parable unto them, Can the blind lead the blind? shall they not both fall into the ditch? **40** The disciple is not above his master: but every one that is perfect shall be as his master. **41** And why beholdest thou the mote that is in thy brother's eye, but perceivest not the beam that is in thine own eye? **42** Either how canst thou say to thy brother, Brother, let me pull out the mote that is in thine eye, when thou thyself beholdest not the beam that is in thine own eye? Thou hypocrite, cast out first the beam out of thine own eye, and then shalt thou see clearly to pull out the mote that is in thy brother's eye. **43** For a good tree bringeth not forth corrupt fruit; neither doth a corrupt tree bring forth good fruit. **44** For every tree is known by his own fruit. For of thorns men do not gather figs, nor of a bramble bush gather they grapes. **45** A good man out of the good treasure of his heart bringeth forth that which is good; and an evil man out of the evil treasure of his heart bringeth forth that which is evil: for of the abundance of the heart his mouth speaketh. **46** And why call ye me, Lord, Lord, and do not the things which I say? **47** Whosoever cometh to me, and heareth my sayings, and doeth them, I will shew you to whom he is like: **48** He is like a man which built an house, and digged deep, and laid the foundation on a rock: and when the flood arose, the stream beat vehemently upon that house, and could not shake it: for it was founded upon a rock. **49** But he that heareth, and doeth not, is like a man that without a foundation built an house upon the earth; against which the stream did beat vehemently, and immediately it fell; and the ruin of that house was great.

Luke 7

Healing the Centurion's Slave

9 When Jesus heard these things, he marvelled at him, and turned him about, and said unto the people that followed him, I say unto you, I have not found so great faith, no, not in Israel.

Raising a Widow's Son

13 And when the Lord saw her, he had compassion on her, and said unto her, Weep not. **14** And he came and touched the bier: and they that bare him stood still. And he said, Young man, I say unto thee, Arise. **15** And he that was dead sat up, and began to speak. And he delivered him to his mother.

Jesus and John the Baptist

22 Then Jesus answering said unto them, Go your way, and tell John what things ye have seen and heard; how that the blind see, the lame walk, the lepers are cleansed, the deaf hear, the dead are raised, to the poor the gospel is preached. 23 And blessed is *he*, whosoever shall not be offended in me. 24 And when the messengers of John were departed, he began to speak unto the people concerning John, What went ye out into the wilderness for to see? A reed shaken with the wind? 25 But what went ye out for to see? A man clothed in soft raiment? Behold, they which are gorgeously apparelled, and live delicately, are in kings' courts. 26 But what went ye out for to see? A prophet? Yea, I say unto you, and much more than a prophet. 27 This is he, of whom it is written, **Behold, I send my messenger before thy face, which shall prepare thy way before thee.** 28 For I say unto you, Among those that are born of women there is not a greater prophet than John the Baptist: but he that is least in the kingdom of God is greater than he. 29 And all the people that heard *him*, and the publicans, justified God, being baptized with the baptism of John. 30 But the Pharisees and lawyers rejected the counsel of God against themselves, being not baptized of him. 31 And the Lord said, Whereunto then shall I liken the men of this generation? and to what are they like? 32 They are like unto children sitting in the marketplace, and calling one to another, and saying, We have piped unto you, and ye have not danced; we have mourned to you, and ye have not wept. 33 For John the Baptist came neither eating bread nor drinking wine; and ye say, He hath a devil. 34 The Son of man is come eating and drinking; and ye say, Behold a gluttonous man, and a winebibber, a friend of publicans and sinners! 35 But wisdom is justified of all her children.

Jesus' Feet Washed with Tears

40 And Jesus answering said unto him, Simon, I have somewhat to say unto thee. And he saith, Master, say on. 41 There was a certain creditor which had two debtors:

the one owed five hundred pence, and the other fifty. **42** And when they had nothing to pay, he frankly forgave them both. Tell me therefore, which of them will love him most? **43** Simon answered and said, I suppose that he, to whom he forgave most. And he said unto him, Thou hast rightly judged. **44** And he turned to the woman, and said unto Simon, Seest thou this woman? I entered into thine house, thou gavest me no water for my feet: but she hath washed my feet with tears, and wiped them with the hairs of her head. **45** Thou gavest me no kiss: but this woman since the time I came in hath not ceased to kiss my feet. **46** My head with oil thou didst not anoint: but this woman hath anointed my feet with ointment. **47** Wherefore I say unto thee, Her sins, which are many, are forgiven; for she loved much: but to whom little is forgiven, the same loveth little. **48** And he said unto her, Thy sins are forgiven. **49** And they that sat at meat with him began to say within themselves, Who is this that forgiveth sins also? **50** And he said to the woman, Thy faith hath saved thee; go in peace.

Luke 8

The Parable of the Sower

4 And when much people were gathered together, and were come to him out of every city, he spake by a parable: **5** A sower went out to sow his seed: and as he sowed, some fell by the way side; and it was trodden down, and the fowls of the air devoured it. **6** And some fell upon a rock; and as soon as it was sprung up, it withered away, because it lacked moisture. **7** And some fell among thorns; and the thorns sprang up with it, and choked it. **8** And other fell on good ground, and sprang up, and bare fruit an hundredfold. And when he had said these things, he cried, He that hath ears to hear, let him hear. **9** And his disciples asked him, saying, What might this parable be? **10** And he said, Unto you it is given to know the mysteries of the kingdom of God: but to others in parables; that

seeing they might not see, and hearing they might not understand. 11 Now the parable is this: The seed is the word of God. 12 Those by the way side are they that hear; then cometh the devil, and taketh away the word out of their hearts, lest they should believe and be saved. 13 They on the rock are they, which, when they hear, receive the word with joy; and these have no root, which for a while believe, and in time of temptation fall away. 14 And that which fell among thorns are they, which, when they have heard, go forth, and are choked with cares and riches and pleasures of this life, and bring no fruit to perfection. 15 But that on the good ground are they, which in an honest and good heart, having heard the word, keep it, and bring forth fruit with patience.

The Candle's Light

16 No man, when he hath lighted a candle, covereth it with a vessel, or putteth it under a bed; but setteth it on a candlestick, that they which enter in may see the light. 17 For nothing is secret, that shall not be made manifest; neither any thing hid, that shall not be known and come abroad. 18 Take heed therefore how ye hear: for whosoever hath, to him shall be given; and whosoever hath not, from him shall be taken even that which he seemeth to have.

The Family of Jesus

21 And he answered and said unto them, My mother and my brethren are these which hear the word of God, and do it.

Jesus Calms the Waters

22 Now it came to pass on a certain day, that he went into a ship with his disciples: and he said unto them, Let us go over unto the other side of the lake. And they launched forth. 23 But as they sailed he fell asleep: and there came down a storm of wind on the lake; and they were filled with water, and were in jeopardy. 24 And they came to him, and awoke him, saying, Master, master, we perish.

Then he arose, and rebuked the wind and the raging of the water: and they ceased, and there was a calm. 25 And he said unto them, Where is your faith? And they being afraid wondered, saying one to another, What manner of man is this! for he commandeth even the winds and water, and they obey him.

Healing of a Demoniac
30 And Jesus asked him, saying, What is thy name? And he said, Legion: because many devils were entered into him. 38 Now the man out of whom the devils were departed besought him that he might be with him: but Jesus sent him away, saying, 39 Return to thine own house, and shew how great things God hath done unto thee. And he went his way, and published throughout the whole city how great things Jesus had done unto him.

Healing of Woman with Issue of Blood
45 And Jesus said, Who touched me? When all denied, Peter and they that were with him said, Master, the multitude throng thee and press thee, and sayest thou, Who touched me? 46 And Jesus said, Somebody hath touched me: for I perceive that virtue is gone out of me. 47 And when the woman saw that she was not hid, she came trembling, and falling down before him, she declared unto him before all the people for what cause she had touched him, and how she was healed immediately. 48 And he said unto her, Daughter, be of good comfort: thy faith hath made thee whole; go in peace.

Jairus' Daughter
49 While he yet spake, there cometh one from the ruler of the synagogue's house, saying to him, Thy daughter is dead; trouble not the Master. 50 But when Jesus heard it, he answered him, saying, Fear not: believe only, and she shall be made whole. 51 And when he came into the house, he suffered no man to go in, save Peter, and James, and John, and the father and the mother of the maiden. 52 And all wept, and bewailed her: but he said, Weep not; she is not

dead, but sleepeth. 53 And they laughed him to scorn, knowing that she was dead. 54 And he put them all out, and took her by the hand, and called, saying, Maid, arise.

Luke 9

The Sending of the Twelve Apostles

2 And he sent them to preach the kingdom of God, and to heal the sick. 3 And he said unto them, Take nothing for your journey, neither staves, nor scrip, neither bread, neither money; neither have two coats apiece. 4 And whatsoever house ye enter into, there abide, and thence depart. 5 And whosoever will not receive you, when ye go out of that city, shake off the very dust from your feet for a testimony against them.

The Feeding of the Five Thousand

13 But he said unto them, Give ye them to eat. And they said, We have no more but five loaves and two fishes; except we should go and buy meat for all this people. 14 For they were about five thousand men. And he said to his disciples, Make them sit down by fifties in a company.

Peter's Confession

18 And it came to pass, as he was alone praying, his disciples were with him: and he asked them, saying, Whom say the people that I am? 19 They answering said, John the Baptist; but some say, Elias; and others say, that one of the old prophets is risen again. 20 He said unto them, But whom say ye that I am? Peter answering said, The Christ of God. 21 And he straitly charged them, and commanded them to tell no man that thing; 22 Saying, The Son of man must suffer many things, and be rejected of the elders and chief priests and scribes, and be slain, and be raised the third day.

A Call to Discipleship

23 And he said to them all, If any man will come after me,

let him deny himself, and take up his cross daily, and follow me. **24** For whosoever will save his life shall lose it: but whosoever will lose his life for my sake, the same shall save it. **25** For what is a man advantaged, if he gain the whole world, and lose himself, or be cast away? **26** For whosoever shall be ashamed of me and of my words, of him shall the Son of man be ashamed, when he shall come in his own glory, and in his Father's, and of the holy angels. **27** But I tell you of a truth, there be some standing here, which shall not taste of death, till they see the kingdom of God.

Healing a Boy with an Unclean Spirit
40 And I besought thy disciples to cast him out; and they could not. **41** And Jesus answering said, O faithless and perverse generation, how long shall I be with you, and suffer you? Bring thy son hither.

Another Prediction of Jesus' Suffering
43 And they were all amazed at the mighty power of God. But while they wondered every one at all things which Jesus did, he said unto his disciples, **44** Let these sayings sink down into your ears: for the Son of man shall be delivered into the hands of men.

The Least to Be the Greatest
47 And Jesus, perceiving the thought of their heart, took a child, and set him by him, **48** And said unto them, Whosoever shall receive this child in my name receiveth me: and whosoever shall receive me receiveth him that sent me: for he that is least among you all, the same shall be great. **49** And John answered and said, Master, we saw one casting out devils in thy name; and we forbad him, because he followeth not with us. **50** And Jesus said unto him, Forbid him not: for he that is not against us is for us.

Rejection in Samaria
54 And when his disciples James and John saw this, they said, Lord, wilt thou that we command fire to come down

from heaven, and consume them, even as Elias did? **55** But he turned, and rebuked them, and said, Ye know not what manner of spirit ye are of. **56** For the Son of man is not come to destroy men's lives, but to save them. And they went to another village.

The High Cost of Discipleship

57 And it came to pass, that, as they went in the way, a certain man said unto him, Lord, I will follow thee whithersoever thou goest. **58** And Jesus said unto him, Foxes have holes, and birds of the air have nests; but the Son of man hath not where to lay his head. **59** And he said unto another, Follow me. But he said, Lord, suffer me first to go and bury my father. **60** Jesus said unto him, Let the dead bury their dead: but go thou and preach the kingdom of God. **61** And another also said, Lord, I will follow thee; but let me first go bid them farewell, which are at home at my house. **62** And Jesus said unto him, No man, having put his hand to the plough, and looking back, is fit for the kingdom of God.

Luke
10

Seventy Labourers Sent Forth

2 Therefore said he unto them, The harvest truly is great, but the labourers are few: pray ye therefore the Lord of the harvest, that he would send forth labourers into his harvest. **3** Go your ways: behold, I send you forth as lambs among wolves. **4** Carry neither purse, nor scrip, nor shoes: and salute no man by the way. **5** And into whatsoever house ye enter, first say, Peace be to this house. **6** And if the son of peace be there, your peace shall rest upon it: if not, it shall turn to you again. **7** And in the same house remain, eating and drinking such things as they give: for the labourer is worthy of his hire. Go not from house to house. **8** And into whatsoever city ye enter, and they receive you, eat such things as are set before you: **9** And heal the sick that are therein, and say unto them, The kingdom of God is come nigh unto you. **10** But into whatsoever city ye enter, and they receive you not, go your ways out into the streets of the same, and say, **11** Even the very dust of your city, which cleaveth on us, we do wipe off against you: notwithstanding be ye sure of this, that the kingdom of God is come nigh unto you. **12** But I say unto you, that it shall be more tolerable in that day for Sodom, than for that city. **13** Woe unto thee, Chorazin! woe unto thee, Bethsaida! for if the mighty works had been done in Tyre and Sidon, which have been done in you, they had a great while ago repented, sitting in sackcloth and ashes. **14** But it shall be more tolerable for Tyre and Sidon at the judgment, than for you. **15** And thou, Capernaum, which art exalted to heaven, shalt be thrust down to hell. **16** He that heareth you heareth me; and he that despiseth you despiseth me; and he that despiseth me despiseth him that sent me.

The Labourer's Joyful Return

17 And the seventy returned again with joy, saying, Lord, even the devils are subject unto us through thy name. **18** And he said unto them, I beheld Satan as lightning fall from heaven. **19** Behold, I give unto you power to tread on serpents and scorpions, and over all the power of the enemy: and nothing shall by any means hurt you. **20** Notwithstanding in this rejoice not, that the spirits are subject unto you; but rather rejoice, because your names are written in heaven. **21** In that hour Jesus rejoiced in spirit, and said, I thank thee, O Father, Lord of heaven and earth, that thou hast hid these things from the wise and prudent, and hast revealed them unto babes: even so, Father; for so it seemed good in thy sight. **22** All things are delivered to me of my Father: and no man knoweth who the Son is, but the Father; and who the Father is, but the Son, and he to whom the Son will reveal him. **23** And he turned him unto his disciples, and said privately, Blessed are the eyes which see the things that ye see: **24** For I tell you, that many prophets and kings have desired to see those things which ye see, and have not seen them; and to hear those things which ye hear, and have not heard them.

The Parable of the Good Samaritan

25 And, behold, a certain lawyer stood up, and tempted him, saying, Master, what shall I do to inherit eternal life? **26** He said unto him, What is written in the law? how readest thou? **27** And he answering said, **Thou shalt love the Lord thy God with all thy heart, and with all thy soul, and with all thy strength, and with all thy mind; and thy neighbour as thyself.** **28** And he said unto him, Thou hast answered right: this do, and thou shalt live. **29** But he, willing to justify himself, said unto Jesus, And who is my neighbour? **30** And Jesus answering said, A certain man went down from Jerusalem to Jericho, and fell among thieves, which stripped him of his raiment, and wounded him, and departed, leaving him half dead. **31** And by chance there came down a certain priest that way: and when he saw him, he passed by on the other side. **32** And likewise a Levite, when he was at the place, came and looked on him, and passed by on the other side. **33** But a certain Samaritan, as he journeyed, came where he was: and when he saw him, he had compassion on him, **34** And went to him, and bound up his wounds, pouring in oil and wine, and set him on his own beast, and brought him to an inn, and took care of him. **35** And on the morrow when he departed, he took out two pence, and gave them to the host, and said unto him, Take care of him; and whatsoever thou spendest more, when I come again, I will repay thee. **36** Which now of these three, thinkest thou, was neighbour unto him that fell among the thieves? **37** And he said, He that shewed mercy on him. Then said Jesus unto him, Go, and do thou likewise.

Martha and Mary

41 And Jesus answered and said unto her, Martha, Martha, thou art careful and troubled about many things: **42** But one thing is needful: and Mary hath chosen that good part, which shall not be taken away from her.

Instructions on Prayer

2 And he said unto them, When ye pray, say, Our Father which art in heaven, Hallowed be thy name. Thy kingdom come. Thy will be done, as in heaven, so in earth. **3** Give us day by day our daily bread. **4** And forgive us our sins; for we also forgive every one that is indebted to us. And lead us not into temptation; but deliver us from evil. **5** And he said unto them, Which of you shall have a friend, and shall go unto him at midnight, and say unto him, Friend, lend me three loaves; **6** For a friend of mine in his journey is come to me, and I have nothing to set before him? **7** And he from within shall answer and say, Trouble me not: the door is now shut, and my children are with me in bed; I cannot rise and give thee. **8** I say unto you, Though he will not rise and give him, because he is his friend, yet because of his importunity he will rise and give him as many as he needeth. **9** And I say unto you, Ask, and it shall be given you; seek, and ye shall find; knock, and it shall be opened unto you. **10** For every one that asketh receiveth; and he that seeketh findeth; and to him that knocketh it shall be opened. **11** If a son shall ask bread of any of you that is a father, will he give him a stone? or if he ask a fish, will he for a fish give him a serpent? **12** Or if he shall ask an egg, will he offer him a scorpion? **13** If ye then, being evil, know how to give good gifts unto your children: how much more shall your heavenly Father give the Holy Spirit to them that ask him?

Jesus and Beelzebul

17 But he, knowing their thoughts, said unto them, Every kingdom divided against itself is brought to desolation; and a house divided against a house falleth. **18** If Satan also be divided against himself, how shall his kingdom stand? because ye say that I cast out devils through

Beelzebub. **19** And if I by Beelzebub cast out devils, by whom do your sons cast them out? therefore shall they be your judges. **20** But if I with the finger of God cast out devils, no doubt the kingdom of God is come upon you. **21** When a strong man armed keepeth his palace, his goods are in peace: **22** But when a stronger than he shall come upon him, and overcome him, he taketh from him all his armour wherein he trusted, and divideth his spoils. **23** He that is not with me is against me: and he that gathereth not with me scattereth. **24** When the unclean spirit is gone out of a man, he walketh through dry places, seeking rest; and finding none, he saith, I will return unto my house whence I came out. **25** And when he cometh, he findeth it swept and garnished. **26** Then goeth he, and taketh to him seven other spirits more wicked than himself; and they enter in, and dwell there: and the last state of that man is worse than the first.

27 And it came to pass, as he spake these things, a certain woman of the company lifted up her voice, and said unto him, Blessed is the womb that bare thee, and the paps which thou hast sucked. **28** But he said, Yea rather, blessed are they that hear the word of God, and keep it.

The Sign of Jonah

29 And when the people were gathered thick together, he began to say, This is an evil generation: they seek a sign; and there shall no sign be given it, but the sign of Jonas the prophet. **30** For as Jonas was a sign unto the Ninevites, so shall also the Son of man be to this generation. **31** The queen of the south shall rise up in the judgment with the men of this generation, and condemn them: for she came from the utmost parts of the earth to hear the wisdom of Solomon; and, behold, a greater than Solomon is here. **32** The men of Nineve shall rise up in the judgment with this generation, and shall condemn it: for they repented at the preaching of Jonas; and, behold, a greater than Jonas *is* here.

The Light of the Body

33 No man, when he hath lighted a candle, putteth it in a secret place, neither under a bushel, but on a candlestick, that they which come in may see the light. **34** The light of the body is the eye: therefore when thine eye is single, thy whole body also is full of light; but when thine eye is evil, thy body also *is* full of darkness. **35** Take heed therefore that the light which is in thee be not darkness. **36** If thy whole body therefore be full of light, having no part dark, the whole shall be full of light, as when the bright shining of a candle doth give thee light.

Jesus Rebukes the Pharisees

39 And the Lord said unto him, Now do ye Pharisees make clean the outside of the cup and the platter; but your inward part is full of ravening and wickedness. **40** Ye fools, did not he that made that which is without make that which is within also? **41** But rather give alms of such things as ye have; and, behold, all things are clean unto you. **42** But woe unto you, Pharisees! for ye tithe mint and rue and all manner of herbs, and pass over judgment and the love of God: these ought ye to have done, and not to leave the other undone. **43** Woe unto you, Pharisees! for ye love the uppermost seats in the synagogues, and greetings in the markets. **44** Woe unto you, scribes and Pharisees, hypocrites! for ye are as graves which appear not, and the men that walk over them are not aware of them.

Jesus Rebukes Lawyers

46 And he said, Woe unto you also, ye lawyers! for ye lade men with burdens grievous to be borne, and ye yourselves touch not the burdens with one of your fingers. **47** Woe unto you! for ye build the sepulchres of the prophets, and your fathers killed them. **48** Truly ye bear witness that ye allow the deeds of your fathers: for they indeed killed them, and ye build their sepulchres. **49** Therefore also said the wisdom of God, I will send them prophets and apostles, and some of them they shall slay and persecute: **50** That the blood of all the prophets, which was shed from the foundation of the world, may be required of this generation; 51 From the blood of Abel unto the blood of Zacharias, which perished between the altar and the temple: verily I say unto you, It shall be required of this generation. 52 Woe unto you, lawyers! for ye have taken away the key of knowledge: ye entered not in yourselves, and them that were entering in ye hindered.

Luke
12

Beware of Hypocrisy

1 In the mean time, when there were gathered together an innumerable multitude of people, insomuch that they trode one upon another, he began to say unto his disciples first of all, Beware ye of the leaven of the Pharisees, which is hypocrisy. 2 For there is nothing covered, that shall not be revealed; neither hid, that shall not be known. 3 Therefore whatsoever ye have spoken in darkness shall be heard in the light; and that which ye have spoken in the ear in closets shall be proclaimed upon the housetops.

Fear God, Not Man

4 And I say unto you my friends, Be not afraid of them that kill the body, and after that have no more that they can do. 5 But I will forewarn you whom ye shall fear: Fear him, which after he hath killed hath power to cast into hell; yea, I say unto you, Fear him. 6 Are not five sparrows sold for two farthings, and not one of them is forgotten before God? 7 But even the very hairs of your head are all numbered. Fear not therefore: ye are of more value than many sparrows. 8 Also I say unto you, Whosoever shall confess me before men, him shall the Son of man also confess before the angels of God: 9 But he that denieth me before men shall be denied before the angels of God. 10 And whosoever shall speak a word against the Son of man, it shall be forgiven him: but unto him that

blasphemeth against the Holy Ghost it shall not be forgiven. **11** And when they bring you unto the synagogues, and unto magistrates, and powers, take ye no thought how or what thing ye shall answer, or what ye shall say: **12** For the Holy Ghost shall teach you in the same hour what ye ought to say.

The Parable of the Rich Landowner

13 And one of the company said unto him, Master, speak to my brother, that he divide the inheritance with me. **14** And he said unto him, Man, who made me a judge or a divider over you? **15** And he said unto them, Take heed, and beware of covetousness: for a man's life consisteth not in the abundance of the things which he possesseth. **16** And he spake a parable unto them, saying, The ground of a certain rich man brought forth plentifully: **17** And he thought within himself, saying, What shall I do, because I have no room where to bestow my fruits? **18** And he said, This will I do: I will pull down my barns, and build greater; and there will I bestow all my fruits and my goods. **19** And I will say to my soul, Soul, thou hast much goods laid up for many years; take thine ease, eat, drink, and be merry. **20** But God said unto him, Thou fool, this night thy soul shall be required of thee: then whose shall those things be, which thou hast provided? **21** So is he that layeth up treasure for himself, and is not rich toward God.

Do Not Worry or Be Fearful

22 And he said unto his disciples, Therefore I say unto you, Take no thought for your life, what ye shall eat; neither for the body, what ye shall put on. **23** The life is more than meat, and the body is more than raiment. **24** Consider the ravens: for they neither sow nor reap; which neither have storehouse nor barn; and God feedeth them: how much more are ye better than the fowls? **25** And which of you with taking thought can add to his stature one cubit? **26** If ye then be not able to do that thing which is least, why take ye thought for the rest? **27** Consider the lilies how they grow: they toil not, they spin not; and yet I say unto you, that Solomon in all his glory was not arrayed like one of these. **28** If then God so clothe the grass, which is to day in the field, and to morrow is cast into the oven; how much more will he clothe you, O ye of little faith? **29** And seek not ye what ye shall eat, or what ye shall drink, neither be ye of doubtful mind. **30** For all these things do the nations of the world seek after: and your Father knoweth that ye have need of these things. **31** But rather seek ye the kingdom of God; and all these things shall be added unto you. **32** Fear not, little flock; for it is your Father's good pleasure to give you the kingdom. **33** Sell that ye have, and give alms; provide yourselves bags which wax not old, a treasure in the heavens that faileth not, where no thief approacheth, neither moth corrupteth. **34** For where your treasure is, there will your heart be also.

Be Watchful

35 Let your loins be girded about, and your lights burning; **36** And ye yourselves like unto men that wait for their lord, when he will return from the wedding; that when he cometh and knocketh, they may open unto him immediately. **37** Blessed are those servants, whom the lord when he cometh shall find watching: verily I say unto you, that he shall gird himself, and make them to sit down to meat, and will come forth and serve them. **38** And if he shall come in the second watch, or come in the third watch, and find them so, blessed are those servants. **39** And this know, that if the goodman of the house had known what hour the thief would come, he would have watched, and not have suffered his house to be broken through. **40** Be ye therefore ready also: for the Son of man cometh at an hour when ye think not.

42 And the Lord said, Who then is that faithful and wise steward, whom his lord shall make ruler over his household, to give them their portion of meat in due season? **43** Blessed is that servant, whom his lord when he cometh shall find so doing. **44** Of a truth I say unto you, that he will make him ruler over all that he hath. **45** But and if that servant say in his heart, My lord delayeth his coming; and shall begin to beat the menservants and maidens, and to eat and drink, and to be drunken; **46** The lord of that servant will come in a day when he looketh not for him, and at an hour when he is not aware, and will cut him in sunder, and will appoint him his portion with the unbelievers. **47** And that servant, which knew his lord's will, and prepared not himself, neither did according to his will, shall be beaten with many stripes. **48** But he that knew not, and did commit things worthy of stripes, shall be beaten with few stripes. For unto whomsoever much is given, of him shall be much required: and to whom men have committed much, of him they will ask the more.

Not Peace, but Division

49 I am come to send fire on the earth; and what will I, if it be already kindled? **50** But I have a baptism to be baptized with; and how am I straitened till it be accomplished! **51** Suppose ye that I am come to give peace on earth? I tell you, Nay; but rather division: **52** For from henceforth there shall be five in one house divided, three against two, and two against three. **53** The father shall be divided against the son, and the son against the father; the mother against the daughter, and the daughter against the mother; the mother in law against her daughter in law, and the daughter in law against her mother in law.

Discerning the Times

54 And he said also to the people, When ye see a cloud rise out of the west, straightway ye say, There cometh a shower; and so it is. **55** And when ye see the south wind blow, ye say, There will be heat; and it cometh to pass. **56** Ye hypocrites, ye can discern the face of the sky and of the earth; but how is it that ye do not discern this time? **57** Yea, and why even of yourselves judge ye not what is right? **58** When thou goest with thine adversary to the magistrate, as thou art in the way, give diligence that thou mayest be delivered from him; lest he hale thee to the judge, and the judge deliver thee to the officer, and the officer cast thee into prison. **59** I tell thee, thou shalt not depart thence, till thou hast paid the very last mite.

Luke
13

A Call to Repent
2 And Jesus answering said unto them, Suppose ye that these Galilaeans were sinners above all the Galilaeans, because they suffered such things? **3** I tell you, Nay: but, except ye repent, ye shall all likewise perish. **4** Or those eighteen, upon whom the tower in Siloam fell, and slew them, think ye that they were sinners above all men that dwelt in Jerusalem? **5** I tell you, Nay: but, except ye repent, ye shall all likewise perish.

Warning to Israel to Bear Fruit
6 He spake also this parable; A certain man had a fig tree planted in his vineyard; and he came and sought fruit thereon, and found none. **7** Then said he unto the dresser of his vineyard, Behold, these three years I come seeking fruit on this fig tree, and find none: cut it down; why cumbereth it the ground? **8** And he answering said unto him, Lord, let it alone this year also, till I shall dig about it, and dung it: **9** And if it bear fruit, well: and if not, then after that thou shalt cut it down.

Healing on the Sabbath
11 And, behold, there was a woman which had a spirit of infirmity eighteen years, and was bowed together, and could in no wise lift up herself. **12** And when Jesus saw her, he called her to him, and said unto her, Woman, thou art loosed from thine infirmity. **13** And he laid his hands on her: and immediately she was made straight, and glorified God. **14** And the ruler of the synagogue answered with indignation, because that Jesus had healed on the

sabbath day, and said unto the people, There are six days in which men ought to work: in them therefore come and be healed, and not on the sabbath day. **15** The Lord then answered him, and said, Thou hypocrite, doth not each one of you on the sabbath loose his ox or his ass from the stall, and lead him away to watering? **16** And ought not this woman, being a daughter of Abraham, whom Satan hath bound, lo, these eighteen years, be loosed from this bond on the sabbath day?

The Kingdom of God

18 Then said he, Unto what is the kingdom of God like? and whereunto shall I resemble it? **19** It is like a grain of mustard seed, which a man took, and cast into his garden; and it grew, and waxed a great tree; and the fowls of the air lodged in the branches of it. **20** And again he said, Whereunto shall I liken the kingdom of God? **21** It is like leaven, which a woman took and hid in three measures of meal, till the whole was leavened.

The Strait Gate

24 Strive to enter in at the strait gate: for many, I say unto you, will seek to enter in, and shall not be able. **25** When once the master of the house is risen up, and hath shut to the door, and ye begin to stand without, and to knock at the door, saying, Lord, Lord, open unto us; and he shall answer and say unto you, I know you not whence ye are: **26** Then shall ye begin to say, We have eaten and drunk in thy presence, and thou hast taught in our streets. **27** But he shall say, I tell you, I know you not whence ye are; depart from me, all ye workers of iniquity. **28** There shall be weeping and gnashing of teeth, when ye shall see Abraham, and Isaac, and Jacob, and all the prophets, in the kingdom of God, and you yourselves thrust out. **29** And they shall come from the east, and from the west, and from the north, and from the south, and shall sit down in the kingdom of God. **30** And, behold, there are last which shall be first, and there are first which shall be last.

Jerusalem 's Desolate House

32 And he said unto them, Go ye, and tell that fox, Behold, I cast out devils, and I do cures to day and to morrow, and the third day I shall be perfected. **33** Nevertheless I must walk to day, and to morrow, and the day following: for it cannot be that a prophet perish out of Jerusalem. **34** O Jerusalem, Jerusalem, which killest the prophets, and stonest them that are sent unto thee; how often would I have gathered thy children together, as a hen doth gather her brood under her wings, and ye would not! **35** Behold, your house is left unto you desolate: and verily I say unto you, Ye shall not see me, until the time come when ye shall say, **Blessed is he that cometh in the name of the Lord.**

Luke
14

Healing Again on the Sabbath

2 And, behold, there was a certain man before him which had the dropsy. **3** And Jesus answering spake unto the lawyers and Pharisees, saying, Is it lawful to heal on the sabbath day? **4** And they held their peace. And he took *him*, and healed him, and let him go; **5** And answered them, saying, Which of you shall have an ass or an ox fallen into a pit, and will not straightway pull him out on the sabbath day?

Seeking Seats of Honour

8 When thou art bidden of any man to a wedding, sit not down in the highest room; lest a more honourable man than thou be bidden of him; **9** And he that bade thee and him come and say to thee, Give this man place; and thou begin with shame to take the lowest room. **10** But when thou art bidden, go and sit down in the lowest room; that when he that bade thee cometh, he may say unto thee, Friend, go up higher: then shalt thou have worship in the presence of them that sit at meat with thee. **11** For whosoever exalteth himself shall be abased; and he that humbleth himself shall be exalted. 12 Then said he also to him that bade him, When thou makest a dinner or a supper, call not thy friends, nor thy brethren, neither thy kinsmen, nor thy rich neighbours; lest they also bid thee again, and a recompence be made thee. 13 But when thou makest a feast, call the poor, the maimed, the lame, the blind: 14 And thou shalt be blessed; for they cannot recompense thee: for thou shalt be recompensed at the resurrection of the just.

The Parable of the Great Supper

15 And when one of them that sat at meat with him heard these things, he said unto him, Blessed is he that shall eat bread in the kingdom of God. 16 Then said he unto him, A certain man made a great supper, and bade many: 17 And sent his servant at supper time to say to them that were bidden, Come; for all things are now ready. 18 And they all with one consent began to make excuse. The first said unto him, I have bought a piece of ground, and I must needs go and see it: I pray thee have me excused. 19 And another said, I have bought five yoke of oxen, and I go to prove them: I pray thee have me excused. 20 And another said, I have married a wife, and therefore I cannot come. 21 So that servant came, and shewed his lord these things. Then the master of the house being angry said to his servant, Go out quickly into the streets and lanes of the city, and bring in hither the poor, and the maimed, and the halt, and the blind. 22 And the servant said, Lord, it is done as thou hast commanded, and yet there is room. 23 And the lord said unto the servant, Go out into the highways and hedges, and compel them to come in, that my house may be filled. 24 For I say unto you, That none of those men which were bidden shall taste of my supper.

The Cost of Discipleship

25 And there went great multitudes with him: and he turned, and said unto them, 26 If any man come to me, and hate not his father, and mother, and wife, and children, and brethren, and sisters, yea, and his own life

also, he cannot be my disciple. **27** And whosoever doth not bear his cross, and come after me, cannot be my disciple. **28** For which of you, intending to build a tower, sitteth not down first, and counteth the cost, whether he have sufficient to finish it? **29** Lest haply, after he hath laid the foundation, and is not able to finish it, all that behold it begin to mock him, **30** Saying, This man began to build, and was not able to finish. **31** Or what king, going to make war against another king, sitteth not down first, and consulteth whether he be able with ten thousand to meet him that cometh against him with twenty thousand? **32** Or else, while the other is yet a great way off, he sendeth an ambassage, and desireth conditions of peace. **33** So likewise, whosoever he be of you that forsaketh not all that he hath, he cannot be my disciple. **34** Salt *is* good: but if the salt have lost his savour, wherewith shall it be seasoned? **35** It is neither fit for the land, nor yet for the dunghill; but men cast it out. He that hath ears to hear, let him hear.

Luke 15

The Parable of the Lost Sheep and Coin

3 And he spake this parable unto them, saying, **4** What man of you, having an hundred sheep, if he lose one of them, doth not leave the ninety and nine in the wilderness, and go after that which is lost, until he find it? **5** And when he hath found it, he layeth it on his shoulders, rejoicing. **6** And when he cometh home, he calleth together his friends and neighbours, saying unto them, Rejoice with me; for I have found my sheep which was lost. **7** I say unto you, that likewise joy shall be in heaven over one sinner that repenteth, more than over ninety and nine just persons, which need no repentance.

8 Either what woman having ten pieces of silver, if she lose one piece, doth not light a candle, and sweep the house, and seek diligently till she find it? **9** And when she hath found it, she calleth her friends and her neighbours together, saying, Rejoice with me; for I have found the piece which I had lost. **10** Likewise, I say unto you, there is joy in the presence of the angels of God over one sinner that repenteth.

The Parable of the Prodigal Son

11 And he said, A certain man had two sons: **12** And the younger of them said to his father, Father, give me the portion of goods that falleth to me. And he divided unto them his living. **13** And not many days after the younger son gathered all together, and took his journey into a far country, and there wasted his substance with riotous living. **14** And when he had spent all, there arose a mighty famine in that land; and he began to be in want. **15** And he went and joined himself to a citizen of that country; and he sent him into his fields to feed swine. **16** And he would fain have filled his belly with the husks that the swine did eat: and no man gave unto him. **17** And when he came to himself, he said, How many hired servants of my father's have bread enough and to spare, and I perish with hunger! **18** I will arise and go to my father, and will say unto him, Father, I have sinned against heaven, and before thee, **19** And am no more worthy to be called thy son: make me as one of thy hired servants. **20** And he arose, and came to his father. But when he was yet a great way off, his father saw him, and had compassion, and ran, and fell on his neck, and kissed him. **21** And the son said unto him, Father, I have sinned against heaven, and in thy sight, and am no more worthy to be called thy son. **22** But the father said to his servants, Bring forth the best robe, and put *it* on him; and put a ring on his hand, and shoes on his feet: **23** And bring hither the fatted calf, and kill it; and let us eat, and be merry: **24** For this my son was dead, and is alive again; he was lost, and is found. And they began to be merry. **25** Now his elder son was in the field: and as he came and drew nigh to the house, he heard music and dancing. **26** And he called one of the servants, and asked what these things meant. **27** And he said unto him, Thy brother is come; and thy father hath killed the fatted calf, because he hath received him safe and sound. 28 And he was angry, and would not go in: therefore came his father out, and intreated him. 29 And he answering said to his father, Lo, these many years do I serve thee, neither transgressed I at any time thy commandment: and yet thou never gavest me a kid, that I might make merry with my friends: 30 But as soon as this thy son was come, which hath devoured thy living with harlots, thou hast killed for him the fatted calf. 31 And he said unto him, Son, thou art ever with me, and all that I have is thine. 32 It was meet that we should make merry, and be glad: for this thy brother was dead, and is alive again; and was lost, and is found.

Luke 16

The Parable of an Unjust Steward

1 And he said also unto his disciples, There was a certain rich man, which had a steward; and the same was accused unto him that he had wasted his goods. 2 And he called him, and said unto him, How is it that I hear this of thee? give an account of thy stewardship; for thou mayest be no longer steward. 3 Then the steward said within himself, What shall I do? for my lord taketh away from me the stewardship: I cannot dig; to beg I am ashamed. 4 I am resolved what to do, that, when I am put out of the stewardship, they may receive me into their houses. 5 So he called every one of his lord's debtors unto him, and said unto the first, How much owest thou unto my lord? 6 And he said, An hundred measures of oil. And he said unto him, Take thy bill, and sit down quickly, and write fifty. 7 Then said he to another, And how much owest thou? And he said, An hundred measures of wheat. And he said unto him, Take thy bill, and write fourscore. 8 And the lord commended the unjust steward, because he had done wisely: for the children of this world are in their generation wiser than the children of light. 9 And I say unto you, Make to yourselves friends of the mammon of

unrighteousness; that, when ye fail, they may receive you into everlasting habitations. **10** He that is faithful in that which is least is faithful also in much: and he that is unjust in the least is unjust also in much. **11** If therefore ye have not been faithful in the unrighteous mammon, who will commit to your trust the true riches? **12** And if ye have not been faithful in that which is another man's, who shall give you that which is your own? **13** No servant can serve two masters: for either he will hate the one, and love the other; or else he will hold to the one, and despise the other. Ye cannot serve God and mammon.

God Knows the Heart

14 And the Pharisees also, who were covetous, heard all these things: and they derided him. **15** And he said unto them, Ye are they which justify yourselves before men; but God knoweth your hearts: for that which is highly esteemed among men is abomination in the sight of God. **16** The law and the prophets were until John: since that time the kingdom of God is preached, and every man presseth into it. **17** And it is easier for heaven and earth to pass, than one tittle of the law to fail. **18** Whosoever putteth away his wife, and marrieth another, committeth adultery: and whosoever marrieth her that is put away from her husband committeth adultery.

The Rich Man and Lazarus

19 There was a certain rich man, which was clothed in purple and fine linen, and fared sumptuously every day: **20** And there was a certain beggar named Lazarus, which was laid at his gate, full of sores, **21** And desiring to be fed with the crumbs which fell from the rich man's table: moreover the dogs came and licked his sores. **22** And it came to pass, that the beggar died, and was carried by the angels into Abraham's bosom: the rich man also died, and was buried; **23** And in hell he lift up his eyes, being in torments, and seeth Abraham afar off, and Lazarus in his bosom. **24** And he cried and said, Father Abraham, have mercy on me, and send Lazarus, that he may dip the tip of his finger in water, and cool my tongue; for I am tormented in this flame. 25 But Abraham said, Son, remember that thou in thy lifetime receivedst thy good things, and likewise Lazarus evil things: but now he is comforted, and thou art tormented. 26 And beside all this, between us and you there is a great gulf fixed: so that they which would pass from hence to you cannot; neither can they pass to us, that would come from thence. 27 Then he said, I pray thee therefore, father, that thou wouldest send him to my father's house: 28 For I have five brethren; that he may testify unto them, lest they also come into this place of torment. 29 Abraham saith unto him, They have Moses and the prophets; let them hear them. 30 And he said, Nay, father Abraham: but if one went unto them from the dead, they will repent. 31 And he said unto him, If they hear not Moses and the prophets, neither will they be persuaded, though one rose from the dead.

Luke
17

Sin, Forgiveness, Faith, and Service

1 Then said he unto the disciples, It is impossible but that offences will come: but woe unto him, through whom they come! 2 It were better for him that a millstone were hanged about his neck, and he cast into the sea, than that he should offend one of these little ones. 3 Take heed to yourselves: If thy brother trespass against thee, rebuke him; and if he repent, forgive him. 4 And if he trespass against thee seven times in a day, and seven times in a day turn again to thee, saying, I repent; thou shalt forgive him. 5 And the apostles said unto the Lord, Increase our faith. 6 And the Lord said, If ye had faith as a grain of mustard seed, ye might say unto this sycamine tree, Be thou plucked up by the root, and be thou planted in the sea; and it should obey you. 7 But which of you, having a servant plowing or feeding cattle, will say unto him by and by, when he is come from the field, Go and sit down

to meat? **8** And will not rather say unto him, Make ready wherewith I may sup, and gird thyself, and serve me, till I have eaten and drunken; and afterward thou shalt eat and drink? **9** Doth he thank that servant because he did the things that were commanded him? I trow not. **10** So likewise ye, when ye shall have done all those things which are commanded you, say, We are unprofitable servants: we have done that which was our duty to do.

The Grateful Leper

14 And when he saw them, he said unto them, Go shew yourselves unto the priests. And it came to pass, that, as they went, they were cleansed. **15** And one of them, when he saw that he was healed, turned back, and with a loud voice glorified God, **16** And fell down on his face at his feet, giving him thanks: and he was a Samaritan. **17** And Jesus answering said, Were there not ten cleansed? but where are the nine? **18** There are not found that returned to give glory to God, save this stranger. **19** And he said unto him, Arise, go thy way: thy faith hath made thee whole.

Teachings on God's Kingdom

20 And when he was demanded of the Pharisees, when the kingdom of God should come, he answered them and said, The kingdom of God cometh not with observation: **21** Neither shall they say, Lo here! or, lo there! for, behold, the kingdom of God is within you. **22** And he said unto the disciples, The days will come, when ye shall desire to see one of the days of the Son of man, and ye shall not see it. **23** And they shall say to you, See here; or, see there: go not after them, nor follow them. **24** For as the lightning, that lighteneth out of the one part under heaven, shineth unto the other part under heaven; so shall also the Son of man be in his day. **25** But first must he suffer many things, and be rejected of this generation. **26** And as it was in the days of Noe, so shall it be also in the days of the Son of man. **27** They did eat, they drank, they married wives, they were given in marriage, until the day that Noe entered into the ark, and the flood came, and destroyed them all. 28 Likewise also as it was in the days of Lot; they did eat, they drank, they bought, they sold, they planted, they builded; 29 But the same day that Lot went out of Sodom it rained fire and brimstone from heaven, and destroyed them all. 30 Even thus shall it be in the day when the Son of man is revealed. 31 In that day, he which shall be upon the housetop, and his stuff in the house, let him not come down to take it away: and he that is in the field, let him likewise not return back. 32 Remember Lot's wife. 33 Whosoever shall seek to save his life shall lose it; and whosoever shall lose his life shall preserve it. 34 I tell you, in that night there shall be two men in one bed; the one shall be taken, and the other shall be left. 35 Two women shall be grinding together; the one shall be taken, and the other left. 36 Two men shall be in the field; the one shall be taken, and the other left. 37 And they answered and said unto him, Where, Lord? And he said unto them, Wheresoever the body is, thither will the eagles be gathered together.

Luke
18

Prayer and the Parable of the Persistent Widow

1 And he spake a parable unto them to this end, that men ought always to pray, and not to faint; 2 Saying, There was in a city a judge, which feared not God, neither regarded man: 3 And there was a widow in that city; and she came unto him, saying, Avenge me of mine adversary. 4 And he would not for a while: but afterward he said within himself, Though I fear not God, nor regard man; 5 Yet because this widow troubleth me, I will avenge her, lest

by her continual coming she weary me. **6** And the Lord said, Hear what the unjust judge saith. **7** And shall not God avenge his own elect, which cry day and night unto him, though he bear long with them? **8** I tell you that he will avenge them speedily. Nevertheless when the Son of man cometh, shall he find faith on the earth?

The Parable of the Pharisee and the Publican
9 And he spake this parable unto certain which trusted in themselves that they were righteous, and despised others: **10** Two men went up into the temple to pray; the one a Pharisee, and the other a publican. **11** The Pharisee stood and prayed thus with himself, God, I thank thee, that I am not as other men are, extortioners, unjust, adulterers, or even as this publican. **12** I fast twice in the week, I give tithes of all that I possess. **13** And the publican, standing afar off, would not lift up so much as his eyes unto heaven, but smote upon his breast, saying, God be merciful to me a sinner. **14** I tell you, this man went down to his house justified rather than the other: for every one that exalteth himself shall be abased; and he that humbleth himself shall be exalted.

Let the Children Come
16 But Jesus called them unto him, and said, Suffer little children to come unto me, and forbid them not: for of such is the kingdom of God. **17** Verily I say unto you, Whosoever shall not receive the kingdom of God as a little child shall in no wise enter therein.

The Wealthy Ruler
18 And a certain ruler asked him, saying, Good Master, what shall I do to inherit eternal life? **19** And Jesus said unto him, Why callest thou me good? none is good, save one, that is, God. **20** Thou knowest the commandments, Do not commit adultery, Do not kill, Do not steal, Do not bear false witness, Honour thy father and thy mother. **21** And he said, All these have I kept from my youth up. **22** Now when Jesus heard these things, he said unto him, Yet

lackest thou one thing: sell all that thou hast, and distribute unto the poor, and thou shalt have treasure in heaven: and come, follow me. 23 And when he heard this, he was very sorrowful: for he was very rich. 24 And when Jesus saw that he was very sorrowful, he said, How hardly shall they that have riches enter into the kingdom of God! 25 For it is easier for a camel to go through a needle's eye, than for a rich man to enter into the kingdom of God. 26 And they that heard it said, Who then can be saved? 27 And he said, The things which are impossible with men are possible with God. 28 Then Peter said, Lo, we have left all, and followed thee. 29 And he said unto them, Verily I say unto you, There is no man that hath left house, or parents, or brethren, or wife, or children, for the kingdom of God's sake, 30 Who shall not receive manifold more in this present time, and in the world to come life everlasting.

Jesus' Coming Death

31 Then he took unto him the twelve, and said unto them, Behold, we go up to Jerusalem, and all things that are written by the prophets concerning the Son of man shall be accomplished. 32 For he shall be delivered unto the Gentiles, and shall be mocked, and spitefully entreated, and spitted on: 33 And they shall scourge him, and put him to death: and the third day he shall rise again.

Jesus Heals a Blind Man

40 And Jesus stood, and commanded him to be brought unto him: and when he was come near, he asked him, 41 Saying, What wilt thou that I shall do unto thee? And he said, Lord, that I may receive my sight. 42 And Jesus said unto him, Receive thy sight: thy faith hath saved thee.

Luke 19

Jesus and Zacchaeus

5 And when Jesus came to the place, he looked up, and

saw him, and said unto him, Zacchaeus, make haste, and come down; for to day I must abide at thy house.

9 And Jesus said unto him, This day is salvation come to this house, forsomuch as he also is a son of Abraham. 10 For the Son of man is come to seek and to save that which was lost.

A Nobleman's Ten Pounds

11 And as they heard these things, he added and spake a parable, because he was nigh to Jerusalem, and because they thought that the kingdom of God should immediately appear. 12 He said therefore, A certain nobleman went into a far country to receive for himself a kingdom, and to return. 13 And he called his ten servants, and delivered them ten pounds, and said unto them, Occupy till I come. 14 But his citizens hated him, and sent a message after him, saying, We will not have this man to reign over us. 15 And it came to pass, that when he was returned, having received the kingdom, then he commanded these servants to be called unto him, to whom he had given the money, that he might know how much every man had gained by trading. 16 Then came the first, saying, Lord, thy pound hath gained ten pounds. 17 And he said unto him, Well, thou good servant: because thou hast been faithful in a very little, have thou authority over ten cities. 18 And the second came, saying, Lord, thy pound hath gained five pounds. 19 And he said likewise to him, Be thou also over five cities. 20 And another came, saying, Lord, behold, here is thy pound, which I have kept laid up in a napkin: 21 For I feared thee, because thou art an austere man: thou takest up that thou layedst not down, and reapest that thou didst not sow. 22 And he saith unto him, Out of thine own mouth will I judge thee, thou wicked servant. Thou knewest that I was an austere man, taking up that I laid not down, and reaping that I did not sow: 23 Wherefore then gavest not thou my money into the bank, that at my coming I might have required mine own with usury? 24 And he said unto them that stood by, Take from him the pound, and give it to him that hath ten pounds.

25 (And they said unto him, Lord, he hath ten pounds.) 26 For I say unto you, That unto every one which hath shall be given; and from him that hath not, even that he hath shall be taken away from him. 27 But those mine enemies, which would not that I should reign over them, bring hither, and slay them before me.

The Triumphal Entry

29 And it came to pass, when he was come nigh to Bethphage and Bethany, at the mount called the mount of Olives, he sent two of his disciples, 30 Saying, Go ye into the village over against you; in the which at your entering ye shall find a colt tied, whereon yet never man sat: loose him, and bring him hither. 31 And if any man ask you, Why do ye loose him? thus shall ye say unto him, Because the Lord hath need of him.

39 And some of the Pharisees from among the multitude said unto him, Master, rebuke thy disciples. 40 And he answered and said unto them, I tell you that, if these should hold their peace, the stones would immediately cry out.

Jesus Weeps for Jerusalem under Judgment

41 And when he was come near, he beheld the city, and wept over it, 42 Saying, If thou hadst known, even thou, at least in this thy day, the things which belong unto thy peace! but now they are hid from thine eyes. 43 For the days shall come upon thee, that thine enemies shall cast a trench about thee, and compass thee round, and keep thee in on every side, 44 And shall lay thee even with the ground, and thy children within thee; and they shall not leave in thee one stone upon another; because thou knewest not the time of thy visitation. 45 And he went into the temple, and began to cast out them that sold therein, and them that bought; 46 Saying unto them, It is written, My house is the house of prayer: but ye have made it a den of thieves.

Jesus' Authority Questioned

2 And spake unto him, saying, Tell us, by what authority doest thou these things? or who is he that gave thee this authority? **3** And he answered and said unto them, I will also ask you one thing; and answer me: **4** The baptism of John, was it from heaven, or of men? **5** And they reasoned with themselves, saying, If we shall say, From heaven; he will say, Why then believed ye him not? **6** But and if we say, Of men; all the people will stone us: for they be persuaded that John was a prophet. **7** And they answered, that they could not tell whence it was. **8** And Jesus said unto them, Neither tell I you by what authority I do these things.

The Lord of the Vineyard

9 Then began he to speak to the people this parable; A certain man planted a vineyard, and let it forth to husbandmen, and went into a far country for a long time. **10** And at the season he sent a servant to the husbandmen, that they should give him of the fruit of the vineyard: but the husbandmen beat him, and sent him away empty. **11** And again he sent another servant: and they beat him also, and entreated him shamefully, and sent him away empty. **12** And again he sent a third: and they wounded him also, and cast him out. **13** Then said the lord of the vineyard, What shall I do? I will send my beloved son: it may be they will reverence him when they see him. **14** But when the husbandmen saw him, they reasoned among themselves, saying, This is the heir: come, let us kill him, that the inheritance may be ours. **15** So they cast him out of the vineyard, and killed him. What therefore shall the lord of the vineyard do unto them? **16** He shall come and destroy these husbandmen, and shall give the vineyard to others. And when they heard *it*, they said, God forbid. **17** And he beheld them, and said, What is this then that is written, **The stone which the builders**

rejected, the same is become the head of the corner?
18 Whosoever shall fall upon that stone shall be broken; but on whomsoever it shall fall, it will grind him to powder.

Paying Tribute to Caesar
22 Is it lawful for us to give tribute unto Caesar, or no? **23** But he perceived their craftiness, and said unto them, Why tempt ye me? **24** Shew me a penny. Whose image and superscription hath it? They answered and said, Caesar's. **25** And he said unto them, Render therefore unto Caesar the things which be Caesar's, and unto God the things which be God's.

Marriage and the Resurrection
34 And Jesus answering said unto them, The children of this world marry, and are given in marriage: **35** But they which shall be accounted worthy to obtain that world, and the resurrection from the dead, neither marry, nor are given in marriage: **36** Neither can they die any more: for they are equal unto the angels; and are the children of God, being the children of the resurrection. **37** Now that the dead are raised, even Moses shewed at the bush, when he calleth the Lord the God of Abraham, and the God of Isaac, and the God of Jacob. **38** For he is not a God of the dead, but of the living: for all live unto him.

The Messiah: David's Son and Lord
41 And he said unto them, How say they that Christ is David's son? **42** And David himself saith in the book of Psalms, **The LORD said unto my Lord, Sit thou on my right hand, 43 Till I make thine enemies thy footstool.** **44** David therefore calleth him Lord, how is he then his son? **45** Then in the audience of all the people he said unto his disciples, **46** Beware of the scribes, which desire to walk in long robes, and love greetings in the markets, and the highest seats in the synagogues, and the chief rooms at feasts; **47** Which devour widows' houses, and for a

shew make long prayers: the same shall receive greater damnation.

Luke
21

A Widow's Sacrificial Offering
1 And he looked up, and saw the rich men casting their gifts into the treasury. 2 And he saw also a certain poor widow casting in thither two mites. 3 And he said, Of a truth I say unto you, that this poor widow hath cast in more than they all: 4 For all these have of their abundance cast in unto the offerings of God: but she of her penury hath cast in all the living that she had.

The Signs of the End of Time
5 And as some spake of the temple, how it was adorned with goodly stones and gifts, he said, 6 As for these things which ye behold, the days will come, in the which there shall not be left one stone upon another, that shall not be thrown down.

Deceivers, Wars, and Disasters
8 And he said, Take heed that ye be not deceived: for many shall come in my name, saying, I am Christ; and the time draweth near: go ye not therefore after them. 9 But when ye shall hear of wars and commotions, be not terrified: for these things must first come to pass; but the end is not by and by. 10 Then said he unto them, Nation shall rise against nation, and kingdom against kingdom: 11 And great earthquakes shall be in divers places, and famines, and pestilences; and fearful sights and great signs shall there be from heaven.

Persecution Will Come
12 But before all these, they shall lay their hands on you, and persecute you, delivering you up to the synagogues, and into prisons, being brought before kings and rulers for my name's sake. 13 And it shall turn to you for a

testimony. **14** Settle it therefore in your hearts, not to meditate before what ye shall answer: **15** For I will give you a mouth and wisdom, which all your adversaries shall not be able to gainsay nor resist. **16** And ye shall be betrayed both by parents, and brethren, and kinsfolks, and friends; and some of you shall they cause to be put to death. **17** And ye shall be hated of all men for my name's sake. **18** But there shall not an hair of your head perish. **19** In your patience possess ye your souls.

The Desolation of Jerusalem

20 And when ye shall see Jerusalem compassed with armies, then know that the desolation thereof is nigh. **21** Then let them which are in Judaea flee to the mountains; and let them which are in the midst of it depart out; and let not them that are in the countries enter thereinto. **22** For these be the days of vengeance, that all things which are written may be fulfilled. **23** But woe unto them that are with child, and to them that give suck, in those days! for there shall be great distress in the land, and wrath upon this people. **24** And they shall fall by the edge of the sword, and shall be led away captive into all nations: and Jerusalem shall be trodden down of the Gentiles, until the times of the Gentiles be fulfilled.

The Arrival of the Son of Man

25 And there shall be signs in the sun, and in the moon, and in the stars; and upon the earth distress of nations, with perplexity; the sea and the waves roaring; **26** Men's hearts failing them for fear, and for looking after those things which are coming on the earth: for the powers of heaven shall be shaken. **27** And then shall they see the Son of man coming in a cloud with power and great glory. **28** And when these things begin to come to pass, then look up, and lift up your heads; for your redemption draweth nigh.

The Parable of the Fig Tree

29 And he spake to them a parable; Behold the fig tree,

and all the trees; **30** When they now shoot forth, ye see and know of your own selves that summer is now nigh at hand. **31** So likewise ye, when ye see these things come to pass, know ye that the kingdom of God is nigh at hand. **32** Verily I say unto you, This generation shall not pass away, till all be fulfilled. **33** Heaven and earth shall pass away: but my words shall not pass away.

Be Ready!

34 And take heed to yourselves, lest at any time your hearts be overcharged with surfeiting, and drunkenness, and cares of this life, and so that day come upon you unawares. **35** For as a snare shall it come on all them that dwell on the face of the whole earth. **36** Watch ye therefore, and pray always, that ye may be accounted worthy to escape all these things that shall come to pass, and to stand before the Son of man.

Luke 22

Passover Preparations

7 Then came the day of unleavened bread, when the passover must be killed. **8** And he sent Peter and John, saying, Go and prepare us the passover, that we may eat. **9** And they said unto him, Where wilt thou that we prepare? **10** And he said unto them, Behold, when ye are entered into the city, there shall a man meet you, bearing a pitcher of water; follow him into the house where he entereth in. **11** And ye shall say unto the goodman of the house, The Master saith unto thee, Where is the guestchamber, where I shall eat the passover with my disciples? **12** And he shall shew you a large upper room furnished: there make ready.

The Lord's Supper

15 And he said unto them, With desire I have desired to eat this passover with you before I suffer: **16** For I say unto you, I will not any more eat thereof, until it be fulfilled in the kingdom of God. **17** And he took the cup, and gave thanks, and said, Take this, and divide it among yourselves: **18** For I say unto you, I will not drink of the fruit of the vine, until the kingdom of God shall come. **19** And he took bread, and gave thanks, and brake *it*, and gave unto them, saying, This is my body which is given for you: this do in remembrance of me. **20** Likewise also the cup after supper, saying, This cup is the new testament in my blood, which is shed for you.

A Final Discourse

21 But, behold, the hand of him that betrayeth me is with me on the table. **22** And truly the Son of man goeth, as it was determined: but woe unto that man by whom he is betrayed! **23** And they began to enquire among themselves, which of them it was that should do this thing. **24** And there was also a strife among them, which of them should be accounted the greatest. **25** And he said unto them, The kings of the Gentiles exercise lordship over them; and they that exercise authority upon them are called benefactors. **26** But ye shall not be so: but he that is greatest among you, let him be as the younger; and he that is chief, as he that doth serve. **27** For whether is greater, he that sitteth at meat, or he that serveth? is not he that sitteth at meat? but I am among you as he that serveth. **28** Ye are they which have continued with me in my temptations. **29** And I appoint unto you a kingdom, as my Father hath appointed unto me; **30** That ye may eat and drink at my table in my kingdom, and sit on thrones judging the twelve tribes of Israel.

Advice for the Disciples

31 And the Lord said, Simon, Simon, behold, Satan hath desired to have you, that he may sift you as wheat: **32** But I have prayed for thee, that thy faith fail not: and when thou art converted, strengthen thy brethren. **33** And he said unto him, Lord, I am ready to go with thee, both into prison, and to death. **34** And he said, I tell thee, Peter, the cock shall not crow this day, before that thou shalt thrice deny that thou knowest me. **35** And he said unto them, When I sent you without purse, and scrip, and shoes, lacked ye any thing? And they said, Nothing. **36** Then said he unto them, But now, he that hath a purse, let him take *it*, and likewise his scrip: and he that hath no sword, let him sell his garment, and buy one. **37** For I say unto you, that this that is written must yet be accomplished in me, **And he was reckoned among the transgressors:** for the things concerning me have an end. **38** And they said, Lord, behold, here are two swords. And he said unto them, It is enough.

Jesus' Agony in Prayer

40 And when he was at the place, he said unto them, Pray that ye enter not into temptation. **41** And he was withdrawn from them about a stone's cast, and kneeled down, and prayed, **42** Saying, Father, if thou be willing, remove this cup from me: nevertheless not my will, but thine, be done.

45 And when he rose up from prayer, and was come to his disciples, he found them sleeping for sorrow, **46** And said unto them, Why sleep ye? rise and pray, lest ye enter into temptation.

Betrayal and Arrest

48 But Jesus said unto him, Judas, betrayest thou the Son of man with a kiss? **49** When they which were about him saw what would follow, they said unto him, Lord, shall we smite with the sword? **50** And one of them smote the servant of the high priest, and cut off his right ear. **51** And Jesus answered and said, Suffer ye thus far. And he touched his ear, and healed him. **52** Then Jesus said unto the chief priests, and captains of the temple, and the elders, which were come to him, Be ye come out, as against a thief, with swords and staves? **53** When I was daily with you in the temple, ye stretched forth no hands against me: but this is your hour, and the power of darkness.

Peter's Denials of Jesus

61 And the Lord turned, and looked upon Peter. And Peter remembered the word of the Lord, how he had said unto him, Before the cock crow, thou shalt deny me thrice.

Jesus Before the Council

67 Art thou the Christ? tell us. And he said unto them, If I tell you, ye will not believe: **68** And if I also ask *you*, ye will not answer me, nor let me go. **69** Hereafter shall the Son of man sit on the right hand of the power of God. **70** Then said they all, Art thou then the Son of God? And he said unto them, Ye say that I am.

Luke 23

Jesus Brought Before Pilate

3 And Pilate asked him, saying, Art thou the King of the Jews? And he answered him and said, Thou sayest it.

Jesus Crucified at Calvary

27 And there followed him a great company of people, and of women, which also bewailed and lamented him. **28** But Jesus turning unto them said, Daughters of Jerusalem, weep not for me, but weep for yourselves, and for your children. **29** For, behold, the days are coming, in the which they shall say, Blessed are the barren, and the wombs that never bare, and the paps which never gave suck. **30** **Then shall they begin to say to the mountains, Fall on us; and to the hills, Cover us.** **31** For if they do these things in a green tree, what shall be done in the dry?

32 And there were also two other, malefactors, led with him to be put to death. **33** And when they were come to the place, which is called Calvary, there they crucified him, and the malefactors, one on the right hand, and the other on the left. **34** Then said Jesus, Father, forgive them; for they know not what they do.

43 And Jesus said unto him, Verily I say unto thee, To day shalt thou be with me in paradise.

46 And when Jesus had cried with a loud voice, he said, Father, **into thy hands I commend my spirit:** and having said thus, he gave up the ghost.

Luke
24

The Resurrection of Jesus

6 He is not here, but is risen: remember how he spake unto you when he was yet in Galilee, **7** Saying, The Son of man must be delivered into the hands of sinful men, and be crucified, and the third day rise again.

Jesus Walks the Road to Emmaus

17 And he said unto them, What manner of communications are these that ye have one to another, as ye walk, and are sad? **18** And the one of them, whose name was Cleopas, answering said unto him, Art thou only a stranger in Jerusalem, and hast not known the things which are come to pass there in these days? **19** And he said unto them, What things? And they said unto him, Concerning Jesus of Nazareth, which was a prophet mighty in deed and word before God and all the people:

25 Then he said unto them, O fools, and slow of heart to believe all that the prophets have spoken: **26** Ought not Christ to have suffered these things, and to enter into his glory?

Jesus' Appearance

36 And as they thus spake, Jesus himself stood in the midst of them, and saith unto them, Peace be unto you. **37** But they were terrified and affrighted, and supposed that they had seen a spirit. **38** And he said unto them, Why are ye troubled? and why do thoughts arise in your hearts? **39** Behold my hands and my feet, that it is I myself: handle me, and see; for a spirit hath not flesh and bones, as ye see me have. **40** And when he had thus spoken, he shewed them his hands and his feet. **41** And while they yet believed not for joy, and wondered, he said unto them, Have ye here any meat? **42** And they gave him a piece of a broiled fish, and of an honeycomb. **43** And he took *it*, and did eat before them.

Jesus' Final Commission

44 And he said unto them, These are the words which I spake unto you, while I was yet with you, that all things must be fulfilled, which were written in the law of Moses, and in the prophets, and *in* the psalms, concerning me. **45** Then opened he their understanding, that they might understand the scriptures, **46** And said unto them, Thus it is written, and thus it behoved Christ to suffer, and to rise from the dead the third day: **47** And that repentance and remission of sins should be preached in his name among all nations, beginning at Jerusalem. **48** And ye are witnesses of these things. **49** And, behold, I send the promise of my Father upon you: but tarry ye in the city of Jerusalem, until ye be endued with power from on high.

John

John 1

Two of John's Disciples Follow Jesus

37 And the two disciples heard him speak, and they followed Jesus. **38** Then Jesus turned, and saw them following, and saith unto them, What seek ye? They said unto him, Rabbi, (which is to say, being interpreted, Master,) where dwellest thou? **39** He saith unto them, Come and see. They came and saw where he dwelt, and abode with him that day: for it was about the tenth hour. **40** One of the two which heard John speak, and followed him, was Andrew, Simon Peter's brother. **41** He first findeth his own brother Simon, and saith unto him, We have found the Messias, which is, being interpreted, the Christ. **42** And he brought him to Jesus. And when Jesus beheld him, he said, Thou art Simon the son of Jona: thou shalt be called Cephas, which is by interpretation, A stone.

The Calling of Philip and Nathanael

43 The day following Jesus would go forth into Galilee, and findeth Philip, and saith unto him, Follow me. **44** Now Philip was of Bethsaida, the city of Andrew and Peter. **45** Philip findeth Nathanael, and saith unto him, We have found him, of whom Moses in the law, and the prophets, did write, Jesus of Nazareth, the son of Joseph. **46** And Nathanael said unto him, Can there any good thing come out of Nazareth? Philip saith unto him, Come and see. **47** Jesus saw Nathanael coming to him, and saith of him, Behold an Israelite indeed, in whom is no guile! **48** Nathanael saith unto him, Whence knowest thou me?

Jesus answered and said unto him, Before that Philip called thee, when thou wast under the fig tree, I saw thee. **49** Nathanael answered and saith unto him, Rabbi, thou art the Son of God; thou art the King of Israel. **50** Jesus answered and said unto him, Because I said unto thee, I saw thee under the fig tree, believest thou? thou shalt see greater things than these. **51** And he saith unto him, Verily, verily, I say unto you, Hereafter ye shall see heaven open, and the angels of God ascending and descending upon the Son of man.

John 2

Jesus Turns Water into Wine

3 And when they wanted wine, the mother of Jesus saith unto him, They have no wine. **4** Jesus saith unto her, Woman, what have I to do with thee? mine hour is not yet come. **5** His mother saith unto the servants, Whatsoever he saith unto you, do it.

7 Jesus saith unto them, Fill the waterpots with water. And they filled them up to the brim. **8** And he saith unto them, Draw out now, and bear unto the governor of the feast. And they bare it. **9** When the ruler of the feast had tasted the water that was made wine, and knew not whence it was: (but the servants which drew the water knew;) the governor of the feast called the bridegroom,

Jesus Cleanses the Temple

16 And said unto them that sold doves, Take these things hence; make not my Father's house an house of merchandise. **17** And his disciples remembered that it was written, **The zeal of thine house hath eaten me up. 18** Then answered the Jews and said unto him, What sign shewest thou unto us, seeing that thou doest these things? **19** Jesus answered and said unto them, Destroy this temple, and in three days I will raise it up.

John 3

Conversation with Nicodemus

3 Jesus answered and said unto him, Verily, verily, I say unto thee, Except a man be born again, he cannot see the kingdom of God. **4** Nicodemus saith unto him, How can a man be born when he is old? can he enter the second time into his mother's womb, and be born? **5** Jesus answered, Verily, verily, I say unto thee, Except a man be born of water and of the Spirit, he cannot enter into the kingdom of God. **6** That which is born of the flesh is flesh; and that which is born of the Spirit is spirit. **7** Marvel not that I said unto thee, Ye must be born again. **8** The wind bloweth where it listeth, and thou hearest the sound thereof, but canst not tell whence it cometh, and whither it goeth: so is every one that is born of the Spirit. **9** Nicodemus answered and said unto him, How can these things be? **10** Jesus answered and said unto him, Art thou a master of Israel, and knowest not these things? **11** Verily, verily, I say unto thee, We speak that we do know, and testify that we have seen; and ye receive not our witness. **12** If I have told you earthly things, and ye believe not, how shall ye believe, if I tell you of heavenly things? **13** And no man hath ascended up to heaven, but he that came down from heaven, even the Son of man which is in heaven. **14** And as Moses lifted up the serpent in the wilderness, even so must the Son of man be lifted up: **15** That whosoever believeth in him should not perish, but have eternal life. **16** For God so loved the world, that he gave his only begotten Son, that whosoever believeth in him should not perish, but have everlasting life. **17** For God sent not his Son into the world to condemn the world; but that the world through him might be saved. **18** He that believeth on him is not condemned: but he that believeth not is condemned already, because he hath not believed in the name of the only begotten Son of God. **19** And this is the condemnation, that light is come into the world, and men loved darkness rather than light, because their deeds were evil. **20** For every one that doeth evil hateth the light, neither cometh to the light, lest his deeds should be reproved. **21** But he that doeth truth cometh to the light, that his deeds may be made manifest, that they are wrought in God.

John 4

Conversation With a Samaritan Woman

7 There cometh a woman of Samaria to draw water: Jesus saith unto her, Give me to drink. **8** (For his disciples were gone away unto the city to buy meat.) **9** Then saith the woman of Samaria unto him, How is it that thou, being a Jew, askest drink of me, which am a woman of Samaria? for the Jews have no dealings with the Samaritans. **10** Jesus answered and said unto her, If thou knewest the gift of God, and who it is that saith to thee, Give me to drink; thou wouldest have asked of him, and he would have given thee living water. **11** The woman saith unto him, Sir, thou hast nothing to draw with, and the well is deep: from whence then hast thou that living water? **12** Art thou greater than our father Jacob, which gave us the well, and drank thereof himself, and his children, and his cattle? **13** Jesus answered and said unto her, Whosoever drinketh of this water shall thirst again: **14** But whosoever drinketh of the water that I shall give him shall never thirst; but the water that I shall give him shall be in him a well of water springing up into everlasting life. **15** The woman saith unto him, Sir, give me this water, that I thirst not, neither come hither to draw. **16** Jesus saith unto her, Go, call thy husband, and come hither. **17** The woman answered and said, I have no husband. Jesus said unto her, Thou hast well said, I have no husband: **18** For thou hast had five husbands; and he whom thou now hast is not thy husband: in that saidst thou truly. **19** The woman saith unto him, Sir, I perceive that thou art a prophet. **20** Our fathers worshipped in this mountain; and ye say, that in Jerusalem is the place where men ought to worship. **21** Jesus saith unto her, Woman, believe me, the hour cometh, when ye shall neither in this mountain, nor yet at Jerusalem, worship the Father. **22** Ye worship ye know not what: we know what we worship: for salvation is of the

Jews. **23** But the hour cometh, and now is, when the true worshippers shall worship the Father in spirit and in truth: for the Father seeketh such to worship him. **24** God is a Spirit: and they that worship him must worship him in spirit and in truth. **25** The woman saith unto him, I know that Messias cometh, which is called Christ: when he is come, he will tell us all things. **26** Jesus saith unto her, I that speak unto thee am he.

The Disciples Return

32 But he said unto them, I have meat to eat that ye know not of. **33** Therefore said the disciples one to another, Hath any man brought him ought to eat? **34** Jesus saith unto them, My meat is to do the will of him that sent me, and to finish his work. **35** Say not ye, There are yet four months, and then cometh harvest? behold, I say unto you, Lift up your eyes, and look on the fields; for they are white already to harvest. **36** And he that reapeth receiveth wages, and gathereth fruit unto life eternal: that both he that soweth and he that reapeth may rejoice together. **37** And herein is that saying true, One soweth, and another reapeth. **38** I sent you to reap that whereon ye bestowed no labour: other men laboured, and ye are entered into their labours.

Jesus Heals a Nobleman's Son

48 Then said Jesus unto him, Except ye see signs and wonders, ye will not believe. **49** The nobleman saith unto him, Sir, come down ere my child die. **50** Jesus saith unto him, Go thy way; thy son liveth. And the man believed the word that Jesus had spoken unto him, and he went his way. **51** And as he was now going down, his servants met him, and told him, saying, Thy son liveth. **52** Then enquired he of them the hour when he began to amend. And they said unto him, Yesterday at the seventh hour the fever left him. **53** So the father knew that it was at the same hour, in the which Jesus said unto him, Thy son liveth: and himself believed, and his whole house.

John 5

Healing a Paralytic at the Pool of Bethesda

6 When Jesus saw him lie, and knew that he had been now a long time in that case, he saith unto him, Wilt thou be made whole? **7** The impotent man answered him, Sir, I have no man, when the water is troubled, to put me into the pool: but while I am coming, another steppeth down before me. **8** Jesus saith unto him, Rise, take up thy bed, and walk. **9** And immediately the man was made whole, and took up his bed, and walked: and on the same day was the sabbath. **10** The Jews therefore said unto him that was cured, It is the sabbath day: it is not lawful for thee to carry thy bed. **11** He answered them, He that made me whole, the same said unto me, Take up thy bed, and walk. **12** Then asked they him, What man is that which said unto thee, Take up thy bed, and walk? **13** And he that was healed wist not who it was: for Jesus had conveyed himself away, a multitude being in that place. **14** Afterward Jesus findeth him in the temple, and said unto him, Behold, thou art made whole: sin no more, lest a worse thing come unto thee.

Responding to Jewish Leaders

17 But Jesus answered them, My Father worketh hitherto, and I work. **18** Therefore the Jews sought the more to kill him, because he not only had broken the sabbath, but said also that God was his Father, making himself equal with God. **19** Then answered Jesus and said unto them, Verily, verily, I say unto you, The Son can do nothing of himself, but what he seeth the Father do: for what things soever he doeth, these also doeth the Son likewise. **20** For the Father loveth the Son, and sheweth him all things that himself doeth: and he will shew him greater works than these, that ye may marvel. **21** For as the Father raiseth up the dead, and quickeneth them; even so the Son quickeneth whom he will. **22** For the Father judgeth no man, but hath committed all judgment unto the Son: **23** That all men should honour the Son, even as they honour the Father. He that honoureth not the Son honoureth not the Father which hath sent him. **24** Verily, verily, I say unto you, He that heareth my word, and believeth on him that sent me, hath everlasting life, and shall not come into condemnation; but is passed from death unto life. **25** Verily, verily, I say unto you, The hour is coming, and now is, when the dead shall hear the voice of the Son of God: and they that hear shall live. **26** For as the Father hath life in himself; so hath he given to the Son to have life in himself; **27** And hath given him authority to execute judgment also, because he is the Son of man. **28** Marvel not at this: for the hour is coming, in the which all that are in the graves shall hear his voice, **29** And shall come forth; they that have done good, unto the resurrection of life; and they that have done evil, unto the resurrection of damnation. **30** I can of mine own self do nothing: as I hear, I judge: and my judgment is just; because I seek not mine own will, but the will of the Father which hath sent me.

More Testimony About Jesus

31 If I bear witness of myself, my witness is not true. **32** There is another that beareth witness of me; and I know that the witness which he witnesseth of me is true. **33** Ye sent unto John, and he bare witness unto the truth. **34** But I receive not testimony from man: but these things I say, that ye might be saved. **35** He was a burning and a shining light: and ye were willing for a season to rejoice in his light. **36** But I have greater witness than that of John: for the works which the Father hath given me to finish, the same works that I do, bear witness of me, that the Father hath sent me. **37** And the Father himself, which hath sent me, hath borne witness of me. Ye have neither heard his voice at any time, nor seen his shape. **38** And ye have not his word abiding in you: for whom he hath sent, him ye believe not. **39** Search the scriptures; for in them ye think ye have eternal life: and they are they which testify of me. **40** And ye will not come to me, that ye might have life. **41** I receive not honour from men. **42** But I know you, that ye have not the love of God in you. **43** I am come in my

Father's name, and ye receive me not: if another shall come in his own name, him ye will receive. **44** How can ye believe, which receive honour one of another, and seek not the honour that cometh from God only? **45** Do not think that I will accuse you to the Father: there is one that accuseth you, even Moses, in whom ye trust. **46** For had ye believed Moses, ye would have believed me: for he wrote of me. **47** But if ye believe not his writings, how shall ye believe my words?

John 6

The Feeding of the Five Thousand

5 When Jesus then lifted up his eyes, and saw a great company come unto him, he saith unto Philip, Whence shall we buy bread, that these may eat? **6** And this he said to prove him: for he himself knew what he would do.

10 And Jesus said, Make the men sit down. Now there was much grass in the place. So the men sat down, in number about five thousand. **11** And Jesus took the loaves; and when he had given thanks, he distributed to the disciples, and the disciples to them that were set down; and likewise of the fishes as much as they would. **12** When they were filled, he said unto his disciples, Gather up the fragments that remain, that nothing be lost.

Jesus Walks on the Sea

19 So when they had rowed about five and twenty or thirty furlongs, they see Jesus walking on the sea, and drawing nigh unto the ship: and they were afraid. **20** But he saith unto them, It is I; be not afraid.

Jesus' Discourse About the Bread of Life

26 Jesus answered them and said, Verily, verily, I say unto you, Ye seek me, not because ye saw the miracles, but because ye did eat of the loaves, and were filled. **27** Labour not for the meat which perisheth, but for that meat which endureth unto everlasting life, which the Son of man shall give unto you: for him hath God the Father sealed.

28 Then said they unto him, What shall we do, that we might work the works of God? **29** Jesus answered and said unto them, This is the work of God, that ye believe on him whom he hath sent. **30** They said therefore unto him, What sign shewest thou then, that we may see, and believe thee? what dost thou work? **31** Our fathers did eat manna in the desert; as it is written, He gave them bread from heaven to eat. **32** Then Jesus said unto them, Verily, verily, I say unto you, Moses gave you not that bread from heaven; but my Father giveth you the true bread from heaven. **33** For the bread of God is he which cometh down from heaven, and giveth life unto the world. **34** Then said they unto him, Lord, evermore give us this bread. **35** And Jesus said unto them, I am the bread of life: he that cometh to me shall never hunger; and he that believeth on me shall never thirst. **36** But I said unto you, That ye also have seen me, and believe not. **37** All that the Father giveth me shall come to me; and him that cometh to me I will in no wise cast out. **38** For I came down from heaven, not to do mine own will, but the will of him that sent me. **39** And this is the Father's will which hath sent me, that of all which he hath given me I should lose nothing, but should raise it up again at the last day. **40** And this is the will of him that sent me, that every one which seeth the Son, and believeth on him, may have everlasting life: and I will raise him up at the last day.

The Murmuring of the Jews

41 The Jews then murmured at him, because he said, I am the bread which came down from heaven. **42** And they said, Is not this Jesus, the son of Joseph, whose father and mother we know? how is it then that he saith, I came down from heaven? **43** Jesus therefore answered and said unto them, Murmur not among yourselves. **44** No man can come to me, except the Father which hath sent me draw him: and I will raise him up at the last day. **45** It is written in the prophets, **And they shall be all taught of God.** Every man therefore that hath heard, and hath learned of the Father, cometh unto me. **46** Not that any man hath seen the Father, save he which is of God, he hath seen the Father. **47** Verily, verily, I say unto you, He that believeth on me hath everlasting life. **48** I am that bread of life. **49** Your fathers did eat manna in the wilderness, and are dead. **50** This is the bread which cometh down from heaven, that a man may eat thereof, and not die. **51** I am the living bread which came down from heaven: if any man eat of this bread, he shall live for ever: and the bread that I will give is my flesh, which I will give for the life of the world. **52** The Jews therefore strove among themselves, saying, How can this man give us his flesh to eat? **53** Then Jesus said unto them, Verily, verily, I say unto you, Except ye eat the flesh of the Son of man, and drink his blood, ye have no life in you. **54** Whoso eateth my flesh, and drinketh my blood, hath eternal life; and I will raise him up at the last day. **55** For my flesh is meat indeed, and my blood is drink indeed. **56** He that eateth my flesh, and drinketh my blood, dwelleth in me, and I in him. **57** As the living Father hath sent me, and I live by the Father: so he that eateth me, even he shall live by me. **58** This is that bread which came down from heaven: not as your fathers did eat manna, and are dead: he that eateth of this bread shall live for ever.

Many Disciples Depart

60 Many therefore of his disciples, when they had heard this, said, This is an hard saying; who can hear it? **61** When Jesus knew in himself that his disciples murmured at it, he said unto them, Doth this offend you? **62** What and if ye shall see the Son of man ascend up where he was before? **63** It is the spirit that quickeneth; the flesh profiteth nothing: the words that I speak unto you, they are spirit, and they are life. **64** But there are some of you that believe not. For Jesus knew from the beginning who they were that believed not, and who should betray him. **65** And he said, Therefore said I unto you, that no man can come unto me, except it were given unto him of my Father. **66** From that time many of his disciples went back, and walked no more with him. **67** Then said Jesus unto the twelve, Will ye also go away? **68** Then Simon Peter answered him, Lord, to whom shall we go? thou hast the words of eternal life. **69** And we believe and are sure that thou art that Christ, the Son of the living God. **70** Jesus answered them, Have not I chosen you twelve, and one of you is a devil?

John 7

The Feast of Tabernacles

6 Then Jesus said unto them, My time is not yet come: but your time is alway ready. **7** The world cannot hate you; but me it hateth, because I testify of it, that the works thereof are evil. **8** Go ye up unto this feast: I go not up yet unto this feast; for my time is not yet full come.

Teaching in the Temple

16 Jesus answered them, and said, My doctrine is not mine, but his that sent me. **17** If any man will do his will, he shall know of the doctrine, whether it be of God, or whether I speak of myself. **18** He that speaketh of himself seeketh his own glory: but he that seeketh his glory that sent him, the same is true, and no unrighteousness is in him. **19** Did not Moses give you the law, and yet none of you keepeth the law? Why go ye about to kill me? **20** The people answered and said, Thou hast a devil: who goeth about to kill thee? **21** Jesus answered and said unto them, I have done one work, and ye all marvel. **22** Moses therefore gave unto you circumcision; (not because it is of Moses, but of the fathers;) and ye on the sabbath day circumcise a man. **23** If a man on the sabbath day receive circumcision, that the law of Moses should not be broken; are ye angry at me, because I have made a man every whit whole on the sabbath day? **24** Judge not according to the appearance, but judge righteous judgment.

Questions About Jesus' Identity

28 Then cried Jesus in the temple as he taught, saying, Ye both know me, and ye know whence I am: and I am not come of myself, but he that sent me is true, whom ye know not. **29** But I know him: for I am from him, and he hath sent me. **30** Then they sought to take him: but no man laid hands on him, because his hour was not yet come. **31** And many of the people believed on him, and said, When Christ cometh, will he do more miracles than these which this man hath done? **32** The Pharisees heard that the people murmured such things concerning him; and the Pharisees and the chief priests sent officers to take him. **33** Then said Jesus unto them, Yet a little while am I with you, and then I go unto him that sent me. **34** Ye shall seek me, and shall not find me: and where I am, thither ye cannot come. **35** Then said the Jews among themselves, Whither will he go, that we shall not find him? will he go unto the dispersed among the Gentiles, and teach the Gentiles? **36** What manner of saying is this that he said, Ye shall seek me, and shall not find me: and where I am, thither ye cannot come?

37 In the last day, that great day of the feast, Jesus stood and cried, saying, If any man thirst, let him come unto me, and drink. **38** He that believeth on me, as the scripture hath said, out of his belly shall flow rivers of living water. **39** (But this spake he of the Spirit, which they that believe on him should receive: for the Holy Ghost was not yet given; because that Jesus was not yet glorified.)

John 8

Jesus Forgives an Adulterous Woman

7 So when they continued asking him, he lifted up himself, and said unto them, He that is without sin among you, let him first cast a stone at her. **8** And again he stooped down, and wrote on the ground.

10 When Jesus had lifted up himself, and saw none but the woman, he said unto her, Woman, where are those thine accusers? hath no man condemned thee? **11** She said, No man, Lord. And Jesus said unto her, Neither do I condemn thee: go, and sin no more.

Jesus as the Light of the World

12 Then spake Jesus again unto them, saying, I am the light of the world: he that followeth me shall not walk in darkness, but shall have the light of life. **13** The Pharisees therefore said unto him, Thou bearest record of thyself; thy record is not true. **14** Jesus answered and said unto them, Though I bear record of myself, yet my record is true: for I know whence I came, and whither I go; but ye cannot tell whence I come, and whither I go. **15** Ye judge after the flesh; I judge no man. **16** And yet if I judge, my judgment is true: for I am not alone, but I and the Father that sent me. **17** It is also written in your law, that the testimony of two men is true. **18** I am one that bear witness of myself, and the Father that sent me beareth witness of me. **19** Then said they unto him, Where is thy Father? Jesus answered, Ye neither know me, nor my Father: if ye had known me, ye should have known my Father also. **20** These words spake Jesus in the treasury, as he taught in the temple: and no man laid hands on him; for his hour was not yet come.

Jesus Speaks for the Father

21 Then said Jesus again unto them, I go my way, and ye shall seek me, and shall die in your sins: whither I go, ye cannot come. **22** Then said the Jews, Will he kill himself? because he saith, Whither I go, ye cannot come. **23** And he said unto them, Ye are from beneath; I am from above: ye are of this world; I am not of this world. **24** I said therefore unto you, that ye shall die in your sins: for if ye believe not that I am he, ye shall die in your sins. **25** Then said they unto him, Who art thou? And Jesus saith unto them, Even the same that I said unto you from the beginning. **26** I have many things to say and to judge of you: but he that sent me is true; and I speak to the world those things which I have heard of him. **27** They understood not that he spake to them of the Father. **28**

Then said Jesus unto them, When ye have lifted up the Son of man, then shall ye know that I am he, and that I do nothing of myself; but as my Father hath taught me, I speak these things. **29** And he that sent me is with me: the Father hath not left me alone; for I do always those things that please him. **30** As he spake these words, many believed on him.

Abraham's Seed

31 Then said Jesus to those Jews which believed on him, If ye continue in my word, then are ye my disciples indeed; **32** And ye shall know the truth, and the truth shall make you free. **33** They answered him, We be Abraham's seed, and were never in bondage to any man: how sayest thou, Ye shall be made free? **34** Jesus answered them, Verily, verily, I say unto you, Whosoever committeth sin is the servant of sin. **35** And the servant abideth not in the house for ever: but the Son abideth ever. **36** If the Son therefore shall make you free, ye shall be free indeed. **37** I know that ye are Abraham's seed; but ye seek to kill me, because my word hath no place in you.

38 I speak that which I have seen with my Father: and ye do that which ye have seen with your father. **39** They answered and said unto him, Abraham is our father. Jesus saith unto them, If ye were Abraham's children, ye would do the works of Abraham. **40** But now ye seek to kill me, a man that hath told you the truth, which I have heard of God: this did not Abraham. **41** Ye do the deeds of your father. Then said they to him, We be not born of fornication; we have one Father, even God. **42** Jesus said unto them, If God were your Father, ye would love me: for I proceeded forth and came from God; neither came I of myself, but he sent me. **43** Why do ye not understand my speech? even because ye cannot hear my word.

The Devil's Children

44 Ye are of your father the devil, and the lusts of your father ye will do. He was a murderer from the beginning, and abode not in the truth, because there is no truth in him. When he speaketh a lie, he speaketh of his own: for he is a liar, and the father of it. **45** And because I tell you the truth, ye believe me not.

46 Which of you convinceth me of sin? And if I say the truth, why do ye not believe me? **47** He that is of God heareth God's words: ye therefore hear them not, because ye are not of God.

Honoured by the Father

49 Jesus answered, I have not a devil; but I honour my Father, and ye do dishonour me. **50** And I seek not mine own glory: there is one that seeketh and judgeth.

51 Verily, verily, I say unto you, If a man keep my saying, he shall never see death. **52** Then said the Jews unto him, Now we know that thou hast a devil. Abraham is dead, and the prophets; and thou sayest, If a man keep my saying, he shall never taste of death. **53** Art thou greater than our father Abraham, which is dead? and the prophets are dead: whom makest thou thyself? **54** Jesus answered, If I honour myself, my honour is nothing: it is my Father that honoureth me; of whom ye say, that he is your God: **55** Yet ye have not known him; but I know him: and if I should say, I know him not, I shall be a liar like unto you: but I know him, and keep his saying. **56** Your father Abraham rejoiced to see my day: and he saw it, and was glad. **57** Then said the Jews unto him, Thou art not yet fifty years old, and hast thou seen Abraham? **58** Jesus said unto them, Verily, verily, I say unto you, Before Abraham was, I am.

John 9

Healing a Man Born Blind

3 Jesus answered, Neither hath this man sinned, nor his parents: but that the works of God should be made manifest in him. **4** I must work the works of him that sent me, while it is day: the night cometh, when no man can work. **5** As long as I am in the world, I am the light of the world. **6** When he had thus spoken, he spat on the ground, and made clay of the spittle, and he anointed the eyes of the blind man with the clay, **7** And said unto him, Go, wash in the pool of Siloam, (which is by interpretation, Sent.) He went his way therefore, and washed, and came seeing. **11** He answered and said, A man that is called Jesus made clay, and anointed mine eyes, and said unto me, Go to the pool of Siloam, and wash: and I went and washed, and I received sight.

The Healed Man Belief

35 Jesus heard that they had cast him out; and when he had found him, he said unto him, Dost thou believe on the Son of God? **36** He answered and said, Who is he, Lord, that I might believe on him? **37** And Jesus said unto him, Thou hast both seen him, and it is he that talketh with thee. **38** And he said, Lord, I believe. And he worshipped him.

39 And Jesus said, For judgment I am come into this world, that they which see not might see; and that they which see might be made blind. **40** And some of the Pharisees which were with him heard these words, and said unto him, Are we blind also? **41** Jesus said unto them, If ye were blind, ye should have no sin: but now ye say, We see; therefore your sin remaineth.

John 10

Jesus as the Good Shepherd

1 Verily, verily, I say unto you, He that entereth not by the door into the sheepfold, but climbeth up some other way, the same is a thief and a robber. **2** But he that entereth in by the door is the shepherd of the sheep. **3** To him the porter openeth; and the sheep hear his voice: and he calleth his own sheep by name, and leadeth them out. **4** And when he putteth forth his own sheep, he goeth before them, and the sheep follow him: for they know his voice. **5** And a stranger will they not follow, but will flee from him: for they know not the voice of strangers. **6** This parable spake Jesus unto them: but they understood not what things they were which he spake unto them. **7** Then said Jesus unto them again, Verily, verily, I say unto you, I am the door of the sheep. **8** All that ever came before me are thieves and robbers: but the sheep did not hear them. **9** I am the door: by me if any man enter in, he shall be saved, and shall go in and out, and find pasture. **10** The thief cometh not, but for to steal, and to kill, and to destroy: I am come that they might have life, and that they might have *it* more abundantly. **11** I am the good shepherd: the good shepherd giveth his life for the sheep. **12** But he that is an hireling, and not the shepherd, whose own the sheep are not, seeth the wolf coming, and leaveth the sheep, and fleeth: and the wolf catcheth them, and scattereth the sheep. **13** The hireling fleeth, because he is an hireling, and careth not for the sheep. **14** I am the good shepherd, and know my sheep, and am known of mine. **15** As the Father knoweth me, even so know I the Father: and I lay down my life for the sheep. **16** And other sheep I have, which are not of this fold: them also I must bring, and they shall hear my voice; and there shall be one fold, and one shepherd. **17** Therefore doth my Father love me, because I lay down my life, that I might take it again. **18** No man taketh it from me, but I lay it down of myself. I have power to lay it down, and I have power to take it again. This commandment have I received of my Father.

Jesus Charged with Blasphemy

25 Jesus answered them, I told you, and ye believed not: the works that I do in my Father's name, they bear witness of me. **26** But ye believe not, because ye are not of my sheep, as I said unto you. **27** My sheep hear my voice, and I know them, and they follow me: **28** And I give unto them eternal life; and they shall never perish, neither shall any man pluck them out of my hand. **29** My Father, which gave them me, is greater than all; and no man is able to pluck them out of my Father's hand. **30** I and my Father are one. **31** Then the Jews took up stones again to stone him. **32** Jesus answered them, Many good works have I shewed you from my Father; for which of those works do ye stone me? **33** The Jews answered him, saying, For a good work we stone thee not; but for blasphemy; and because that thou, being a man, makest thyself God. **34** Jesus answered them, Is it not written in your law, **I said, Ye are gods? 35** If he called them gods, unto whom the word of God came, and the scripture cannot be broken; **36** Say ye of him, whom the Father hath sanctified, and sent into the world, Thou blasphemest; because I said, I am the Son of God? **37** If I do not the works of my Father, believe me not. **38** But if I do, though ye believe not me, believe the works: that ye may know, and believe, that the Father is in me, and I in him.

John 11

The Death of Lazarus

4 When Jesus heard that, he said, This sickness is not unto death, but for the glory of God, that the Son of God might be glorified thereby. **5** Now Jesus loved Martha, and her sister, and Lazarus. **6** When he had heard therefore that he was sick, he abode two days still in the same place where he was. **7** Then after that saith he to his disciples, Let us go into Judaea again. **8** His disciples say unto him, Master, the Jews of late sought to stone thee; and goest thou thither again? **9** Jesus answered, Are there not twelve hours in the day? If any man walk in the day, he stumbleth not, because he seeth the light of this world. **10** But if a man walk in the night, he stumbleth, because there is no light in him. **11** These things said he: and after that he saith unto them, Our friend Lazarus sleepeth; but I go, that I may awake him out of sleep. **12** Then said his disciples, Lord, if he sleep, he shall do well. **13** Howbeit Jesus spake of his death: but they thought that he had spoken of taking of rest in sleep. **14** Then said Jesus unto them plainly, Lazarus is dead. **15** And I am glad for your sakes that I was not there, to the intent ye may believe; nevertheless let us go unto him.

Martha's Assurance of the Resurrection

23 Jesus saith unto her, Thy brother shall rise again. **24** Martha saith unto him, I know that he shall rise again in the resurrection at the last day. **25** Jesus said unto her, I am the resurrection, and the life: he that believeth in me, though he were dead, yet shall he live: **26** And whosoever liveth and believeth in me shall never die. Believest thou this?

Jesus Raises Lazarus from the Dead

39 Jesus said, Take ye away the stone. Martha, the sister of him that was dead, saith unto him, Lord, by this time he stinketh: for he hath been dead four days. **40** Jesus saith unto her, Said I not unto thee, that, if thou wouldest believe, thou shouldest see the glory of God? **41** Then they took away the stone from the place where the dead was laid. And Jesus lifted up his eyes, and said, Father, I thank thee that thou hast heard me. **42** And I knew that thou hearest me always: but because of the people which stand by I said it, that they may believe that thou hast sent me. **43** And when he thus had spoken, he cried with a loud voice, Lazarus, come forth. **44** And he that was dead came forth, bound hand and foot with graveclothes: and his face was bound about with a napkin. Jesus saith unto them, Loose him, and let him go.

John 12

Mary Anoints the Feet of Jesus

7 Then said Jesus, Let her alone: against the day of my burying hath she kept this. **8** For the poor always ye have with you; but me ye have not always.

The Son of Man to be Glorified

23 And Jesus answered them, saying, The hour is come, that the Son of man should be glorified. **24** Verily, verily, I say unto you, Except a corn of wheat fall into the ground and die, it abideth alone: but if it die, it bringeth forth much fruit. **25** He that loveth his life shall lose it; and he that hateth his life in this world shall keep it unto life eternal. **26** If any man serve me, let him follow me; and where I am, there shall also my servant be: if any man serve me, him will my Father honour.

27 Now is my soul troubled; and what shall I say? Father, save me from this hour: but for this cause came I unto this hour. **28** Father, glorify thy name. Then came there a voice from heaven, saying, I have both glorified it, and will glorify it again. **29** The people therefore, that stood by, and heard *it*, said that it thundered: others said, An angel spake to him. **30** Jesus answered and said, This voice came not because of me, but for your sakes. **31** Now is the judgment of this world: now shall the prince of this world be cast out. **32** And I, if I be lifted up from the earth, will draw all men unto me. **33** This he said, signifying what death he should die. **34** The people answered him, We have heard out of the law that Christ abideth for ever: and how sayest thou, The Son of man must be lifted up? who is this Son of man? **35** Then Jesus said unto them, Yet a little while is the light with you. Walk while ye have the light, lest darkness come upon you: for he that walketh in darkness knoweth not whither he goeth. **36** While ye have light, believe in the light, that ye may be the children of light. These things spake Jesus, and departed, and did hide himself from them.

Jesus' Final Public Words

44 Jesus cried and said, He that believeth on me, believeth not on me, but on him that sent me. **45** And he that seeth me seeth him that sent me. **46** I am come a light into the world, that whosoever believeth on me should not abide in darkness. **47** And if any man hear my words, and believe not, I judge him not: for I came not to judge the world, but to save the world. **48** He that rejecteth me, and receiveth not my words, hath one that judgeth him: the word that I have spoken, the same shall judge him in the last day. **49** For I have not spoken of myself; but the

Father which sent me, he gave me a commandment, what I should say, and what I should speak. **50** And I know that his commandment is life everlasting: whatsoever I speak therefore, even as the Father said unto me, so I speak.

John 13

Jesus Washes the Disciples' Feet

7 Jesus answered and said unto him, What I do thou knowest not now; but thou shalt know hereafter. **8** Peter saith unto him, Thou shalt never wash my feet. Jesus answered him, If I wash thee not, thou hast no part with me. **9** Simon Peter saith unto him, Lord, not my feet only, but also my hands and my head. **10** Jesus saith to him, He that is washed needeth not save to wash his feet, but is clean every whit: and ye are clean, but not all. **11** For he knew who should betray him; therefore said he, Ye are not all clean. **12** So after he had washed their feet, and had taken his garments, and was set down again, he said unto them, Know ye what I have done to you? **13** Ye call me Master and Lord: and ye say well; for so I am. **14** If I then, your Lord and Master, have washed your feet; ye also ought to wash one another's feet. **15** For I have given you an example, that ye should do as I have done to you. **16** Verily, verily, I say unto you, The servant is not greater than his lord; neither he that is sent greater than he that sent him. **17** If ye know these things, happy are ye if ye do them.

Preparing for His Betrayal

18 I speak not of you all: I know whom I have chosen: but that the scripture may be fulfilled, **He that eateth bread with me hath lifted up his heel against me. 19** Now I tell you before it come, that, when it is come to pass, ye may believe that I am he. **20** Verily, verily, I say unto you, He that receiveth whomsoever I send receiveth me; and he that receiveth me receiveth him that sent me. **21** When Jesus had thus said, he was troubled in spirit, and testified, and said, Verily, verily, I say unto you, that one of you shall betray me. 22 Then the disciples looked one on another, doubting of whom he spake. 23 Now there was leaning on Jesus' bosom one of his disciples, whom Jesus loved. 24 Simon Peter therefore beckoned to him, that he should ask who it should be of whom he spake. 25 He then lying on Jesus' breast saith unto him, Lord, who is it? 26 Jesus answered, He it is, to whom I shall give a sop, when I have dipped it. And when he had dipped the sop, he gave *it* to Judas Iscariot, the son of Simon. 27 And after the sop Satan entered into him. Then said Jesus unto him, That thou doest, do quickly.

Peter to Deny Jesus

31 Therefore, when he was gone out, Jesus said, Now is the Son of man glorified, and God is glorified in him. 32 If God be glorified in him, God shall also glorify him in himself, and shall straightway glorify him. 33 Little children, yet a little while I am with you. Ye shall seek me: and as I said unto the Jews, Whither I go, ye cannot come; so now I say to you. 34 A new commandment I give unto you, That ye love one another; as I have loved you, that ye also love one another. 35 By this shall all men know that ye are my disciples, if ye have love one to another.

36 Simon Peter said unto him, Lord, whither goest thou? Jesus answered him, Whither I go, thou canst not follow me now; but thou shalt follow me afterwards. 37 Peter said unto him, Lord, why cannot I follow thee now? I will lay down my life for thy sake. 38 Jesus answered him, Wilt thou lay down thy life for my sake? Verily, verily, I say unto thee, The cock shall not crow, till thou hast denied me thrice.

John 14

Jesus' Parting Words to His Disciples

1 Let not your heart be troubled: ye believe in God, believe also in me. 2 In my Father's house are many mansions: if it were not so, I would have told you. I go to prepare a place for you. 3 And if I go and prepare a place

for you, I will come again, and receive you unto myself; that where I am, there ye may be also.

4 And whither I go ye know, and the way ye know. 5 Thomas saith unto him, Lord, we know not whither thou goest; and how can we know the way? 6 Jesus saith unto him, I am the way, the truth, and the life: no man cometh unto the Father, but by me. 7 If ye had known me, ye should have known my Father also: and from henceforth ye know him, and have seen him. 8 Philip saith unto him, Lord, shew us the Father, and it sufficeth us. 9 Jesus saith unto him, Have I been so long time with you, and yet hast thou not known me, Philip? he that hath seen me hath seen the Father; and how sayest thou then, Shew us the Father? 10 Believest thou not that I am in the Father, and the Father in me? the words that I speak unto you I speak not of myself: but the Father that dwelleth in me, he doeth the works. 11 Believe me that I am in the Father, and the Father in me: or else believe me for the very works' sake.

12 Verily, verily, I say unto you, He that believeth on me, the works that I do shall he do also; and greater works than these shall he do; because I go unto my Father. 13 And whatsoever ye shall ask in my name, that will I do, that the Father may be glorified in the Son. 14 If ye shall ask any thing in my name, I will do it.

A Comforter Will Come

15 If ye love me, keep my commandments. 16 And I will pray the Father, and he shall give you another Comforter, that he may abide with you for ever; 17 Even the Spirit of truth; whom the world cannot receive, because it seeth him not, neither knoweth him: but ye know him; for he dwelleth with you, and shall be in you.

18 I will not leave you comfortless: I will come to you. 19 Yet a little while, and the world seeth me no more; but ye see me: because I live, ye shall live also. 20 At that day ye shall know that I am in my Father, and ye in me, and I in you. 21 He that hath my commandments, and keepeth them, he it is that loveth me: and he that loveth me shall

be loved of my Father, and I will love him, and will manifest myself to him. **22** Judas saith unto him, not Iscariot, Lord, how is it that thou wilt manifest thyself unto us, and not unto the world? **23** Jesus answered and said unto him, If a man love me, he will keep my words: and my Father will love him, and we will come unto him, and make our abode with him. **24** He that loveth me not keepeth not my sayings: and the word which ye hear is not mine, but the Father's which sent me.

25 These things have I spoken unto you, being yet present with you. **26** But the Comforter, which is the Holy Ghost, whom the Father will send in my name, he shall teach you all things, and bring all things to your remembrance, whatsoever I have said unto you. **27** Peace I leave with you, my peace I give unto you: not as the world giveth, give I unto you. Let not your heart be troubled, neither let it be afraid.

28 Ye have heard how I said unto you, I go away, and come again unto you. If ye loved me, ye would rejoice, because I said, I go unto the Father: for my Father is greater than I. **29** And now I have told you before it come to pass, that, when it is come to pass, ye might believe. **30** Hereafter I will not talk much with you: for the prince of this world cometh, and hath nothing in me. **31** But that the world may know that I love the Father; and as the Father gave me commandment, even so I do. Arise, let us go hence.

John 15

The Vine and the Branches

1 I am the true vine, and my Father is the husbandman. **2** Every branch in me that beareth not fruit he taketh away: and every branch that beareth fruit, he purgeth it, that it may bring forth more fruit. **3** Now ye are clean through the word which I have spoken unto you. **4** Abide in me, and I in you. As the branch cannot bear fruit of itself, except it abide in the vine; no more can ye, except ye abide in me. **5** I am the vine, ye are the branches: He that abideth in me, and I in him, the same bringeth forth much fruit: for without me ye can do nothing. **6** If a man abide not in me, he is cast forth as a branch, and is withered; and men gather them, and cast them into the fire, and they are burned. **7** If ye abide in me, and my words abide in you, ye shall ask what ye will, and it shall be done unto you. **8** Herein is my Father glorified, that ye bear much fruit; so shall ye be my disciples.

9 As the Father hath loved me, so have I loved you: continue ye in my love. **10** If ye keep my commandments, ye shall abide in my love; even as I have kept my Father's commandments, and abide in his love. **11** These things have I spoken unto you, that my joy might remain in you, and that your joy might be full. **12** This is my commandment, That ye love one another, as I have loved you. **13** Greater love hath no man than this, that a man lay down his life for his friends. **14** Ye are my friends, if ye do whatsoever I command you. **15** Henceforth I call you not servants; for the servant knoweth not what his lord doeth: but I have called you friends; for all things that I have heard of my Father I have made known unto you. **16** Ye have not chosen me, but I have chosen you, and ordained you, that ye should go and bring forth fruit, and that your fruit should remain: that whatsoever ye shall ask of the Father in my name, he may give it you. **17** These things I command you, that ye love one another.

The World Will Hate Jesus' Follower

18 If the world hate you, ye know that it hated me before it hated you. **19** If ye were of the world, the world would love his own: but because ye are not of the world, but I have chosen you out of the world, therefore the world hateth you. **20** Remember the word that I said unto you, The servant is not greater than his lord. If they have persecuted me, they will also persecute you; if they have kept my saying, they will keep yours also. **21** But all these things will they do unto you for my name's sake, because they know not him that sent me. **22** If I had not come and spoken unto them, they had not had sin: but now they have no cloke for their sin. 23 He that hateth me hateth my Father also. 24 If I had not done among them the works which none other man did, they had not had sin: but now have they both seen and hated both me and my Father. 25 But this cometh to pass, that the word might be fulfilled that is written in their law, **They hated me without a cause.**

26 But when the Comforter is come, whom I will send unto you from the Father, even the Spirit of truth, which proceedeth from the Father, he shall testify of me: 27 And ye also shall bear witness, because ye have been with me from the beginning.

John 16

Words of Warning

1 These things have I spoken unto you, that ye should not be offended. 2 They shall put you out of the synagogues: yea, the time cometh, that whosoever killeth you will think that he doeth God service. 3 And these things will they do unto you, because they have not known the Father, nor me. 4 But these things have I told you, that when the time shall come, ye may remember that I told you of them. And these things I said not unto you at the beginning, because I was with you. 5 But now I go my way to him that sent me; and none of you asketh me, Whither goest thou? 6 But because I have said these things unto you, sorrow hath filled your heart.

7 Nevertheless I tell you the truth; It is expedient for you that I go away: for if I go not away, the Comforter will not come unto you; but if I depart, I will send him unto you. 8 And when he is come, he will reprove the world of sin, and of righteousness, and of judgment:*2* 9 Of sin, because they believe not on me; 10 Of righteousness, because I go to my Father, and ye see me no more; 11 Of judgment, because the prince of this world is judged. 12 I have yet many things to say unto you, but ye cannot bear them now. 13 Howbeit when he, the Spirit of truth, is come, he will guide you into all truth: for he shall not speak of

himself; but whatsoever he shall hear, that shall he speak: and he will shew you things to come. **14** He shall glorify me: for he shall receive of mine, and shall shew it unto you. **15** All things that the Father hath are mine: therefore said I, that he shall take of mine, and shall shew it unto you.

16 A little while, and ye shall not see me: and again, a little while, and ye shall see me, because I go to the Father.

Your Sorrows will Turn to Joy

17 Then said some of his disciples among themselves, What is this that he saith unto us, A little while, and ye shall not see me: and again, a little while, and ye shall see me: and, Because I go to the Father? **18** They said therefore, What is this that he saith, A little while? we cannot tell what he saith. **19** Now Jesus knew that they were desirous to ask him, and said unto them, Do ye enquire among yourselves of that I said, A little while, and ye shall not see me: and again, a little while, and ye shall see me? **20** Verily, verily, I say unto you, That ye shall weep and lament, but the world shall rejoice: and ye shall be sorrowful, but your sorrow shall be turned into joy. **21** A woman when she is in travail hath sorrow, because her hour is come: but as soon as she is delivered of the child, she remembereth no more the anguish, for joy that a man is born into the world. **22** And ye now therefore have sorrow: but I will see you again, and your heart shall rejoice, and your joy no man taketh from you.

23 And in that day ye shall ask me nothing. Verily, verily, I say unto you, Whatsoever ye shall ask the Father in my name, he will give it you. **24** Hitherto have ye asked nothing in my name: ask, and ye shall receive, that your joy may be full. **25** These things have I spoken unto you in proverbs: but the time cometh, when I shall no more speak unto you in proverbs, but I shall shew you plainly of the Father. **26** At that day ye shall ask in my name: and I say not unto you, that I will pray the Father for you: **27** For the Father himself loveth you, because ye have loved me, and have believed that I came out from God.

28 I came forth from the Father, and am come into the world: again, I leave the world, and go to the Father. **29** His disciples said unto him, Lo, now speakest thou plainly, and speakest no proverb. **30** Now are we sure that thou knowest all things, and needest not that any man should ask thee: by this we believe that thou camest forth from God. **31** Jesus answered them, Do ye now believe? **32** Behold, the hour cometh, yea, is now come, that ye shall be scattered, every man to his own, and shall leave me alone: and yet I am not alone, because the Father is with me. **33** These things I have spoken unto you, that in me ye might have peace. In the world ye shall have tribulation: but be of good cheer; I have overcome the world.

John 17

Jesus Prayer for Himself

1 These words spake Jesus, and lifted up his eyes to heaven, and said, Father, the hour is come; glorify thy Son, that thy Son also may glorify thee: **2** As thou hast given him power over all flesh, that he should give eternal life to as many as thou hast given him. **3** And this is life eternal, that they might know thee the only true God, and Jesus Christ, whom thou hast sent. **4** I have glorified thee on the earth: I have finished the work which thou gavest me to do. **5** And now, O Father, glorify thou me with thine own self with the glory which I had with thee before the world was.

Jesus' Prayer for His Disciples

6 I have manifested thy name unto the men which thou gavest me out of the world: thine they were, and thou gavest them me; and they have kept thy word. **7** Now they have known that all things whatsoever thou hast given me are of thee. **8** For I have given unto them the words which thou gavest me; and they have received them, and have known surely that I came out from thee, and they have believed that thou didst send me. **9** I pray for them: I pray not for the world, but for them which thou hast given me; for they are thine. **10** And all mine are thine, and thine are mine; and I am glorified in them.

11 And now I am no more in the world, but these are in the world, and I come to thee. Holy Father, keep through thine own name those whom thou hast given me, that they may be one, as we are. **12** While I was with them in the world, I kept them in thy name: those that thou gavest me I have kept, and none of them is lost, but the son of perdition; that the scripture might be fulfilled. **13** And now come I to thee; and these things I speak in the world, that they might have my joy fulfilled in themselves. **14** I have given them thy word; and the world hath hated them, because they are not of the world, even as I am not of the world. **15** I pray not that thou shouldest take them out of the world, but that thou shouldest keep them from the evil. **16** They are not of the world, even as I am not of the world.

17 Sanctify them through thy truth: thy word is truth. **18** As thou hast sent me into the world, even so have I also sent them into the world. **19** And for their sakes I sanctify myself, that they also might be sanctified through the truth.

Jesus' Prayer for Believers

20 Neither pray I for these alone, but for them also which shall believe on me through their word; **21** That they all may be one; as thou, Father, art in me, and I in thee, that they also may be one in us: that the world may believe that thou hast sent me. **22** And the glory which thou gavest me I have given them; that they may be one, even as we are one: **23** I in them, and thou in me, that they may be made perfect in one; and that the world may know that thou hast sent me, and hast loved them, as thou hast loved me.

24 Father, I will that they also, whom thou hast given me, be with me where I am; that they may behold my glory, which thou hast given me: for thou lovedst me before the foundation of the world. **25** O righteous Father, the world hath not known thee: but I have known thee, and these have known that thou hast sent me. **26** And I have declared unto them thy name, and will declare it: that the love wherewith thou hast loved me may be in them, and I in them.

John 18

Betrayal and Arrest

4 Jesus therefore, knowing all things that should come upon him, went forth, and said unto them, Whom seek ye? **5** They answered him, Jesus of Nazareth. Jesus saith unto them, I am he. And Judas also, which betrayed him, stood with them. **6** As soon then as he had said unto them, I am he, they went backward, and fell to the ground. **7** Then asked he them again, Whom seek ye? And they said, Jesus of Nazareth. **8** Jesus answered, I have told you that I am he: if therefore ye seek me, let these go their way: **9** That the saying might be fulfilled, which he spake, Of them which thou gavest me have I lost none. **10** Then Simon Peter having a sword drew it, and smote the high priest's servant, and cut off his right ear. The servant's name was Malchus. **11** Then said Jesus unto Peter, Put up thy sword into the sheath: the cup which my Father hath given me, shall I not drink it?

Jesus Questioned About His Doctrine

20 Jesus answered him, I spake openly to the world; I ever taught in the synagogue, and in the temple, whither the Jews always resort; and in secret have I said nothing. **21** Why askest thou me? ask them which heard me, what I have said unto them: behold, they know what I said. **22** And when he had thus spoken, one of the officers which stood by struck Jesus with the palm of his hand, saying, Answerest thou the high priest so? **23** Jesus answered him, If I have spoken evil, bear witness of the evil: but if well, why smitest thou me?

Pilate Questions Jesus

33 Then Pilate entered into the judgment hall again, and called Jesus, and said unto him, Art thou the King of the Jews? **34** Jesus answered him, Sayest thou this thing of thyself, or did others tell it thee of me? **35** Pilate answered, Am I a Jew? Thine own nation and the chief priests have delivered thee unto me: what hast thou done? **36** Jesus answered, My kingdom is not of this world: if my kingdom were of this world, then would my servants fight, that I should not be delivered to the Jews: but now is my kingdom not from hence. **37** Pilate therefore said unto him, Art thou a king then? Jesus answered, Thou sayest that I am a king. To this end was I born, and for this cause came I into the world, that I should bear witness unto the truth. Every one that is of the truth heareth my voice.

John 19

Jesus is Scourged and Mocked
10 Then saith Pilate unto him, Speakest thou not unto me? knowest thou not that I have power to crucify thee, and have power to release thee? **11** Jesus ánswered, Thou couldest have no power at all against me, except it were given thee from above: therefore he that delivered me unto thee hath the greater sin.

Jesus is crucified at Golgotha
26 When Jesus therefore saw his mother, and the disciple standing by, whom he loved, he saith unto his mother, Woman, behold thy son! **27** Then saith he to the disciple, Behold thy mother! And from that hour that disciple took her unto his own home. **28** After this, Jesus knowing that all things were now accomplished, that the scripture might be fulfilled, saith, I thirst. **29** Now there was set a vessel full of vinegar: and they filled a spunge with vinegar, and put it upon hyssop, and put it to his mouth. **30** When Jesus therefore had received the vinegar, he said, It is finished: and he bowed his head, and gave up the ghost.

John 20

Mary Magdalene Sees Jesus

15 Jesus saith unto her, Woman, why weepest thou? whom seekest thou? She, supposing him to be the gardener, saith unto him, Sir, if thou have borne him hence, tell me where thou hast laid him, and I will take him away. **16** Jesus saith unto her, Mary. She turned herself, and saith unto him, Rabboni; which is to say, Master. **17** Jesus saith unto her, Touch me not; for I am not yet ascended to my Father: but go to my brethren, and say unto them, I ascend unto my Father, and your Father; and to my God, and your God.

The Disciples See Jesus

19 Then the same day at evening, being the first day of the week, when the doors were shut where the disciples were assembled for fear of the Jews, came Jesus and stood in the midst, and saith unto them, Peace be unto you. **20** And when he had so said, he shewed unto them his hands and his side. Then were the disciples glad, when they saw the Lord. **21** Then said Jesus to them again, Peace be unto you: as my Father hath sent me, even so send I you. **22** And when he had said this, he breathed on them, and saith unto them, Receive ye the Holy Ghost: **23** Whose soever sins ye remit, they are remitted unto them; and whose soever sins ye retain, they are retained.

Thomas Sees Jesus

26 And after eight days again his disciples were within, and Thomas with them: then came Jesus, the doors being shut, and stood in the midst, and said, Peace be unto you. **27** Then saith he to Thomas, Reach hither thy finger, and behold my hands; and reach hither thy hand, and thrust it into my side: and be not faithless, but believing. **28** And Thomas answered and said unto him, My Lord and my

God. **29** Jesus saith unto him, Thomas, because thou hast seen me, thou hast believed: blessed are they that have not seen, and yet have believed.

John 21

Jesus' Appearance to the Disciples in Galilee

5 Then Jesus saith unto them, Children, have ye any meat? They answered him, No. **6** And he said unto them, Cast the net on the right side of the ship, and ye shall find. They cast therefore, and now they were not able to draw it for the multitude of fishes.

10 Jesus saith unto them, Bring of the fish which ye have now caught. **11** Simon Peter went up, and drew the net to land full of great fishes, an hundred and fifty and three: and for all there were so many, yet was not the net broken. **12** Jesus saith unto them, Come and dine. And none of the disciples durst ask him, Who art thou? knowing that it was the Lord.

Peter's Restoration

15 So when they had dined, Jesus saith to Simon Peter, Simon, son of Jonas, lovest thou me more than these? He saith unto him, Yea, Lord; thou knowest that I love thee. He saith unto him, Feed my lambs. **16** He saith to him again the second time, Simon, son of Jonas, lovest thou me? He saith unto him, Yea, Lord; thou knowest that I love thee. He saith unto him, Feed my sheep. **17** He saith unto him the third time, Simon, son of Jonas, lovest thou me? Peter was grieved because he said unto him the third time, Lovest thou me? And he said unto him, Lord, thou knowest all things; thou knowest that I love thee. Jesus saith unto him, Feed my sheep. **18** Verily, verily, I say unto thee, When thou wast young, thou girdedst thyself, and walkedst whither thou wouldest: but when thou shalt be old, thou shalt stretch forth thy hands, and another shall gird thee, and carry thee whither thou wouldest not. **19** This spake he, signifying by what death he should glorify God. And when he had spoken this, he saith unto him,

Follow me.

20 Then Peter, turning about, seeth the disciple whom Jesus loved following; which also leaned on his breast at supper, and said, Lord, which is he that betrayeth thee? 21 Peter seeing him saith to Jesus, Lord, and what shall this man do? 22 Jesus saith unto him, If I will that he tarry till I come, what is that to thee? follow thou me. 23 Then went this saying abroad among the brethren, that that disciple should not die: yet Jesus said not unto him, He shall not die; but, If I will that he tarry till I come, what is that to thee?

Acts

Acts 1
Wait for the Promise of the Father
4 And, being assembled together with them, commanded them that they should not depart from Jerusalem, but wait for the promise of the Father, which, saith he, ye have heard of me. **5** For John truly baptized with water; but ye shall be baptized with the Holy Ghost not many days hence.

6 When they therefore were come together, they asked of him, saying, Lord, wilt thou at this time restore again the kingdom to Israel? **7** And he said unto them, It is not for you to know the times or the seasons, which the Father hath put in his own power. **8** But ye shall receive power, after that the Holy Ghost is come upon you: and ye shall be witnesses unto me both in Jerusalem, and in all Judaea, and in Samaria, and unto the uttermost part of the earth.

Acts 9
The Conversion of Saul
4 And he fell to the earth, and heard a voice saying unto him, Saul, Saul, why persecutest thou me? **5** And he said, Who art thou, Lord? And the Lord said, I am Jesus whom thou persecutest: it is hard for thee to kick against the pricks. **6** And he trembling and astonished said, Lord, what wilt thou have me to do? And the Lord said unto him, Arise, and go into the city, and it shall be told thee what thou must do.

Ananias and Saul
10 And there was a certain disciple at Damascus, named

Ananias; and to him said the Lord in a vision, Ananias. And he said, Behold, I am here, Lord. 11 And the Lord said unto him, Arise, and go into the street which is called Straight, and enquire in the house of Judas for one called Saul, of Tarsus: for, behold, he prayeth, 12 And hath seen in a vision a man named Ananias coming in, and putting his hand on him, that he might receive his sight. 13 Then Ananias answered, Lord, I have heard by many of this man, how much evil he hath done to thy saints at Jerusalem: 14 And here he hath authority from the chief priests to bind all that call on thy name. 15 But the Lord said unto him, Go thy way: for he is a chosen vessel unto me, to bear my name before the Gentiles, and kings, and the children of Israel: 16 For I will shew him how great things he must suffer for my name's sake.

Acts 11

Jewish Believers Challenge Peter
16 Then remembered I the word of the Lord, how that he said, John indeed baptized with water; but ye shall be baptized with the Holy Ghost.

Acts 18

Paul Completes His Journey
9 Then spake the Lord to Paul in the night by a vision, Be not afraid, but speak, and hold not thy peace: 10 For I am with thee, and no man shall set on thee to hurt thee: for I have much people in this city.

Acts 20

Paul Calls the Ephesian Elders
35 I have shewed you all things, how that so labouring ye ought to support the weak, and to remember the words of the Lord Jesus, how he said, It is more blessed to give than to receive.

Acts 22

Saul Meets the Lord

7 And I fell unto the ground, and heard a voice saying unto me, Saul, Saul, why persecutest thou me? **8** And I answered, Who art thou, Lord? And he said unto me, I am Jesus of Nazareth, whom thou persecutest. **9** And they that were with me saw indeed the light, and were afraid; but they heard not the voice of him that spake to me. **10** And I said, What shall I do, Lord? And the Lord said unto me, Arise, and go into Damascus; and there it shall be told thee of all things which are appointed for thee to do.

God's Choice of a Witness

18 And saw him saying unto me, Make haste, and get thee quickly out of Jerusalem: for they will not receive thy testimony concerning me. **19** And I said, Lord, they know that I imprisoned and beat in every synagogue them that believed on thee: **20** And when the blood of thy martyr Stephen was shed, I also was standing by, and consenting unto his death, and kept the raiment of them that slew him. **21** And he said unto me, Depart: for I will send thee far hence unto the Gentiles.

Acts 23

Paul Addresses the Council

11 And the night following the Lord stood by him, and said, Be of good cheer, Paul: for as thou hast testified of me in Jerusalem, so must thou bear witness also at Rome.

Acts 26

Paul Describes His Conversion

14 And when we were all fallen to the earth, I heard a voice speaking unto me, and saying in the Hebrew tongue, Saul, Saul, why persecutest thou me? it is hard for thee to kick against the pricks. **15** And I said, Who art thou, Lord? And he said, I am Jesus whom thou persecutest. **16** But rise, and stand upon thy feet: for I have appeared unto thee for this purpose, to make thee a minister and a witness both of these things which thou hast seen, and of those things in the which I will appear unto thee; **17** Delivering thee from the people, and from the Gentiles, unto whom now I send thee, **18** To open their eyes, and to turn them from darkness to light, and from the power of Satan unto God, that they may receive forgiveness of sins, and inheritance among them which are sanctified by faith that is in me.

1 Corinthians

---

1 Corinthians 11
The Lord's Supper

24 And when he had given thanks, he brake it, and said, Take, eat: this is my body, which is broken for you: this do in remembrance of me. **25** After the same manner also he took the cup, when he had supped, saying, This cup is the new testament in my blood: this do ye, as oft as ye drink *it*, in remembrance of me.

2 Corinthians 12
The Lord's Supper

9 My grace is sufficient for thee, for my strength is made perfect in weakness.

Revelation

Revelation 1
Greetings to the Seven Churches
8 I am Alpha and Omega, the beginning and the ending, saith the Lord, which is, and which was, and which is to come, the Almighty.

The Alpha and Omega
10 I was in the Spirit on the Lord's day, and heard behind me a great voice, as of a trumpet, **11** Saying, I am Alpha and Omega, the first and the last: and, What thou seest, write in a book, and send *it* unto the seven churches which are in Asia; unto Ephesus, and unto Smyrna, and unto Pergamos, and unto Thyatira, and unto Sardis, and unto Philadelphia, and unto Laodicea.

17 And when I saw him, I fell at his feet as dead. And he laid his right hand upon me, saying unto me, Fear not; **I am the first and the last: 18** I am he that liveth, and was dead; and, behold, I am alive for evermore, Amen; and have the keys of hell and of death. **19** Write the things which thou hast seen, and the things which are, and the things which shall be hereafter; **20** The mystery of the seven stars which thou sawest in my right hand, and the seven golden candlesticks. The seven stars are the angels of the seven churches: and the seven candlesticks which thou sawest are the seven churches.

Revelation 2

To the Church in Ephesus

1 Unto the angel of the church of Ephesus write; These things saith he that holdeth the seven stars in his right hand, who walketh in the midst of the seven golden candlesticks; **2** I know thy works, and thy labour, and thy patience, and how thou canst not bear them which are evil: and thou hast tried them which say they are apostles, and are not, and hast found them liars: **3** And hast borne, and hast patience, and for my name's sake hast laboured, and hast not fainted. **4** Nevertheless I have somewhat against thee, because thou hast left thy first love. **5** Remember therefore from whence thou art fallen, and repent, and do the first works; or else I will come unto thee quickly, and will remove thy candlestick out of his place, except thou repent. **6** But this thou hast, that thou hatest the deeds of the Nicolaitans, which I also hate. **7** He that hath an ear, let him hear what the Spirit saith unto the churches; To him that overcometh will I give to eat of the tree of life, which is in the midst of the paradise of God.

To the Church in Smyrna

8 And unto the angel of the church in Smyrna write; These things saith the first and the last, which was dead, and is alive; **9** I know thy works, and tribulation, and poverty, (but thou art rich) and I know the blasphemy of them which say they are Jews, and are not, but are the synagogue of Satan. **10** Fear none of those things which thou shalt suffer: behold, the devil shall cast some of you into prison, that ye may be tried; and ye shall have tribulation ten days: be thou faithful unto death, and I will give thee a crown of life. **11** He that hath an ear, let him hear what the Spirit saith unto the churches; He that overcometh shall not be hurt of the second death.

To the Church in Pergamos

12 And to the angel of the church in Pergamos write; These things saith he which hath the sharp sword with two edges; **13** I know thy works, and where thou dwellest, even where Satan's seat is: and thou holdest fast my name, and hast not denied my faith, even in those days wherein Antipas was my faithful martyr, who was slain among you, where Satan dwelleth. **14** But I have a few things against thee, because thou hast there them that hold the doctrine of Balaam, who taught Balac to cast a stumblingblock before the children of Israel, to eat things sacrificed unto idols, and to commit fornication. **15** So hast thou also them that hold the doctrine of the Nicolaitans, which thing I hate. **16** Repent; or else I will come unto thee quickly, and will fight against them with the sword of my mouth. **17** He that hath an ear, let him hear what the Spirit saith unto the churches; To him that overcometh will I give to eat of the hidden manna, and will give him a white stone, and in the stone a new name written, which no man knoweth saving he that receiveth it.

To the Church in Thyatira

18 And unto the angel of the church in Thyatira write; These things saith the Son of God, who hath his eyes like unto a flame of fire, and his feet are like fine brass; **19** I know thy works, and charity, and service, and faith, and thy patience, and thy works; and the last to be more than the first. **20** Notwithstanding I have a few things against thee, because thou sufferest that woman Jezebel, which calleth herself a prophetess, to teach and to seduce my servants to commit fornication, and to eat things sacrificed unto idols. **21** And I gave her space to repent of her fornication; and she repented not. **22** Behold, I will cast her into a bed, and them that commit adultery with her into great tribulation, except they repent of their deeds. **23** And I will kill her children with death; and all the churches shall know that **I am he which searcheth the reins and hearts: and I will give unto every one of you according to your works.** **24** But unto you I say, and unto the rest in Thyatira, as many as have not this doctrine, and which have not known the depths of Satan, as they speak; I will put upon you none other burden. **25**

But that which ye have already hold fast till I come. **26** And he that overcometh, and keepeth my works unto the end, to him will I give power over the nations: **27 And he shall rule them with a rod of iron; as the vessels of a potter shall they be broken to shivers:** even as I received of my Father. **28** And I will give him the morning star. **29** He that hath an ear, let him hear what the Spirit saith unto the churches.

Revelation 3

To the Church in Sardis

1 And unto the angel of the church in Sardis write; These things saith he that hath the seven Spirits of God, and the seven stars; I know thy works, that thou hast a name that thou livest, and art dead. **2** Be watchful, and strengthen the things which remain, that are ready to die: for I have not found thy works perfect before God. **3** Remember therefore how thou hast received and heard, and hold fast, and repent. If therefore thou shalt not watch, I will come on thee as a thief, and thou shalt not know what hour I will come upon thee. **4** Thou hast a few names even in Sardis which have not defiled their garments; and they shall walk with me in white: for they are worthy. **5** He that overcometh, the same shall be clothed in white raiment; and I will not blot out his name out of the book of life, but I will confess his name before my Father, and before his angels. **6** He that hath an ear, let him hear what the Spirit saith unto the churches.

To the Church in Philadelphia

7 And to the angel of the church in Philadelphia write; These things saith he that is holy, he that is true, **he that hath the key of David, he that openeth, and no man shutteth; and shutteth, and no man openeth; 8** I know thy works: behold, I have set before thee an open door, and no man can shut it: for thou hast a little strength, and hast kept my word, and hast not denied my name. **9** Behold, I will make them of the synagogue of Satan, which say they are Jews, and are not, but do lie; behold, I will make them to come and worship before thy feet, and to know that I have loved thee. **10** Because thou hast kept the word of my patience, I also will keep thee from the hour of temptation, which shall come upon all the world, to try them that dwell upon the earth. **11** Behold, I come quickly: hold that fast which thou hast, that no man take thy crown. **12** Him that overcometh will I make a pillar in the temple of my God, and he shall go no more out: and I will write upon him the name of my God, and the name of the city of my God, which is new Jerusalem, which cometh down out of heaven from my God: and I will write upon him my new name. **13** He that hath an ear, let him hear what the Spirit saith unto the churches.

To the Church in Laodicea

14 And unto the angel of the church of the Laodiceans write; These things saith the Amen, the faithful and true witness, the beginning of the creation of God; **15** I know thy works, that thou art neither cold nor hot: I would thou wert cold or hot. **16** So then because thou art lukewarm, and neither cold nor hot, I will spue thee out of my mouth. **17** Because thou sayest, I am rich, and increased with goods, and have need of nothing; and knowest not that thou art wretched, and miserable, and poor, and blind, and naked: **18** I counsel thee to buy of me gold tried in the fire, that thou mayest be rich; and white raiment, that thou mayest be clothed, and that the shame of thy nakedness do not appear; and anoint thine eyes with eyesalve, that thou mayest see. **19** As many as I love, I rebuke and chasten: be zealous therefore, and repent. **20** Behold, I stand at the door, and knock: if any man hear my voice, and open the door, I will come in to him, and will sup with him, and he with me. **21** To him that overcometh will I grant to sit with me in my throne, even as I also overcame, and am set down with my Father in his throne. **22** He that hath an ear, let him hear what the Spirit saith unto the churches.

Revelation 16

The Seven Vials of God's Wrath

15 Behold, I come as a thief. Blessed is he that watcheth, and keepeth his garments, lest he walk naked, and they see his shame.

Revelation 22

Jesus Will Come Quickly

7 Behold, I come quickly: blessed is he that keepeth the sayings of the prophecy of this book.

12 And, behold, I come quickly; and my reward is with me, to give every man according as his work shall be. **13** I am Alpha and Omega, the beginning and the end, the first and the last.

16 I Jesus have sent mine angel to testify unto you these things in the churches. I am the root and the offspring of David, and the bright and morning star.

20 He which testifieth these things saith, Surely I come quickly. Amen. Even so, come, Lord Jesus.

Guide Through the book

MATHEW

LUKE

176

JOHN